DRAGONS DO IT NERDIER

A DRAGON SHIFTERS DO IT ROMANCE

GEMMA CATES

ABOUT DRAGONS DO IT NERDIER

A blocked writer looking for inspiration

Kaylee

I write about bad men who do dirty things to needy women. Or I *used* to.

I'm on a deadline and the words aren't coming. My creative well is nothing more than a mud puddle. Perhaps a reflection of my equally uninspiring life.

But then I encounter a smoking man with a serious book habit at my local library. Suddenly, *he's* my hero.

I'm writing about a gorgeous, bespectacled guy with lickable abs and bitable biceps.

The words are flowing, but it's not the book I meant to write. Not enough handcuffs, too many teeth and claws...and I'm not entirely sure why.

A nerdy dragon looking for love
Dex
I found her. My one true mate. And...
She thinks I'm a lunatic.
"Dragons aren't real."

I just have to convince a woman with an imagination so vast she creates fictional worlds for a living that everything she's ever dreamt is real, magic included.
No problem.

Without revealing my true form.
More complicated.

While keeping her safe from my enemies.
Dammit.

Note from the author: This book contains a practical writer who's certain that dreams and magic are for children, and that happily-ever-after only exists in fiction. It also contains a badass nerd dragon who's ready for love...until he meets the woman of his dreams and realizes life with him is full of unavoidable dangers.

ALSO BY GEMMA CATES

Almost Human Vampire Romance

I Wanna Suck Your (Becca & Simon)

I Wanna Bite Your (Megan & Oliver)

I Wanna Lick Your (Yvette)

I Wanna Nibble Your (Kayla)

Van Helsing Sisters Adventures

A Touch of Wild (Mariah Van Helsing)

A Touch of Crazy (Mia Van Helsing)

A Touch of Wicked (Morgan Van Helsing)

A Touch of Sin (Tilly Van Helsing)

A Touch of Monster Hunter Romance (Collection)

Dragon Shifters Do It

Dragons Do It Dirtier

Dragons Do It Nerdier

Dragons Do It Naughtier

For the most up-to-date list of Gemma's books, visit:

www.GemmaCates.com

OF DRAGONS AND DRAGONKIND: A CURSED LINEAGE

All dragon shifters were men.

It hadn't always been so.

At some point in a long distant past, dragonkind had been like most other magical creatures, with both males and females born in roughly equal numbers.

But for many centuries now, only male children born of a dragon mating were true dragon shifters, possessing the duality of dragon and man inside them. A female child of a dragon mating took the aspect of her mother.

Lore claimed a male dragon betrayed his mate, a dragoness who was also a powerful witch. Her heart shattered by the deceitful actions of her unfaithful mate, she'd used her own death to power a spell. She magicked dragonkind, her intent to spare its females the desolation of an unnaturally broken mate bond.

What had been a blessing in her eyes, saving all other dragonesses from the despair she'd suffered, became a curse to all dragonkind as fewer and fewer females were born until eventually none remained.

Dragons were forced to look elsewhere to find their mates.

For a brief time, dragons embraced this solution. But it didn't take long for dragon males to discover that there were very few creatures with whom they could create a mating bond.

As more time passed, civilizations grew and mankind spread across the planet.

Already declining in number, dragonkind faced a new challenge: concealment from the eyes of mankind.

With their numbers diminishing, the only dragons left were those descended from lineages capable of cloaking themselves from the nonmagical.

And they could only thrive if they could find mates.

So they searched...

1

KAYLEE

The guy was here again.

The gorgeous one with all the muscles and the glasses.

He was hard to miss, since most guys at my local library branch were either teenagers or octogenarians...but I also might have been looking for him.

I might have started coming to the library every morning to write instead of my usual once or twice a week. Well, to write, and in hopes of getting a glimpse of him and all his pretty muscles.

Not that I was a weirdo stalker or anything. I didn't follow him out of the library to see what kind of car he drove. Or try to figure out what books he was reading. That would be creepy.

No, I just...looked.

I swallowed a wistful sigh. He was yummy. Inspirationally, mouthwateringly, motivationally yummy.

A lightbulb flickered.

My latest book had stalled. I felt like I was trudging through a sticky mire of useless words. The blinking cursor taunted me with its wink-wink-wink, as if with each flash it was poking me. "You suck. You suck. You suck."

A word of warning to my future self: shaking the computer didn't work. And drinking a gallon of coffee might be an even worse choice. In fact, all that caffeine made me twitch in time to the vicious jibes of my cursor.

I had a schedule, and no words were coming. My outline was lame. My hero unfun. What was worse, even I didn't want to do my character. If I didn't want to get cuffed, spanked, and fucked by the guy, why bother writing about him at all? Because if I didn't want him, no one reading the damn book would either.

Unlike my library hottie.

Who wouldn't want to read about him?

And that was when not just a lightbulb but stadium lighting went off in my head.

My nerdy hottie was a man born to be a romance hero.

I could make that happen.

The hero in my book morphed. He turned into the gorgeous bespectacled guy with ridiculously fabulous muscles, and the words started to flow.

DEX

My hot stalker was at the library again.

I noticed her last week and was intrigued. She was an adorable bunch of contradictions. Hot as fuck but wrapped in an oversized beige cardigan I'd swear I saw my eighty-two-year-old neighbor wearing the other day.

Interested—she'd eye-fucked me every time she didn't think I was looking her way—but wouldn't make eye contact.

And absolutely oblivious to the fact that I was onto her.

She eyed me like she wanted to yank me into the travel section and suck my dick until I blew my load. How was I *not* supposed to notice that?

But I played along. I let her maintain the delusion that she wasn't obviously checking me out.

Mostly because the alternative wasn't great. She seemed shy enough with the no-eye-contact business to pack up, disappear, and not come back if she realized she'd been found out.

So I watched her watch me, and I watched her type frantically on her laptop. I wasn't sure why she was in the library every morning, because she certainly wasn't here for the books.

Unlike me. I glanced at the pile I'd made atop my favorite reading table. I had research to do. Sort of. I wasn't going to find answers to a magical problem in a human library, but I was hoping for some hints that would point me in the direction I should be looking.

My buddy Bain thought I'd lost my mind. He was ready to knock a few heads together locally and get some answers, but I wasn't so sure that was the most productive route. For one, neither of us knew where to start. It wasn't like I'd pissed off a witch who'd then hexed me.

To the best of my knowledge, I'd only been around three witches recently. Aiden, the ice witch who was buddies with Bain and wouldn't even consider messing with one of us.

Then there was the Van Helsing who could throw fire. No way I'd pissed off Morgan Van Helsing, and if I had, she'd have told me to my face then tried to set me on fire. End of story. She was straight-forward like that.

As for the third one, I didn't think she even knew she was a witch. That was some weird. Bain's woman's ex's fling was a witch. The few times I'd run into her at Derek's, my initial suspicion had been reaffirmed: witch. Oblivious, probably an accident waiting to happen, but definitely a witch.

Aiden was Bain's friend, and neither of those ladies had a beef with me, and there weren't any other fucking witches. Especially not the kind of beef that bound my dragon, preventing me from shifting.

Cue the angry internal dragon roar. Not really. But sort of. The inner calm I worked at was definitely being tested. I was a dragon shifter who couldn't shift. Not ideal, but not panic-worthy—or so I was telling the big guy who made up my beastly half. And it was even true, so long as I didn't get into any fights, need my fire, or need to heal.

If it lasted more than a few weeks, then I'd be ready to fuck up some people in pursuit of answers. I was still a big guy who knew how to fight. As it was, it was an inconvenience. It wasn't like I flew around in cloaked dragon form on a nightly basis.

Eventually it would be a problem, because I had to shift regularly. Stretch my wings, let loose of the fiery badass beast inside me. Man, I was already missing it, and it hadn't been a week yet.

Hence my morning library outings. I was here to find answers, not scope out my sexy stalker.

Okay, fine. I was here for both reasons. I could multitask. I was clever that way.

I glanced over the top of the book on modern myths and witchcraft that I was reading.

My stalker's hair looked long, but I was only guessing. It was all wrapped up in a messy swirl of chocolate strands with bits of honey sticking out. She was a hot, adorable mess.

She shifted in her seat, which was her tell. She was about to glance my way. I pushed my newly acquired glasses high on the bridge of my nose, ducked my head, and pretended to be absorbed by the text. Surreptitiously, I watched her over the tops of my readers. With my chin tucked in, I could just see her.

Thankfully, my distance vision was intact. It was only my close vision that had been affected by the hex.

I was of the opinion that my situation, both my shifting issue and the other effects I'd been experiencing, were temporary. There was no way I'd angered a witch powerful enough to bind my dragon for any significant duration. Not without realizing it.

Temporary was good. I could be patient. Except...

The other symptoms involved were troubling. Those I hadn't shared with Bain or Archer. Those guys might be my best friends, but they'd either lose their shit or give me shit, depending on their mood, and I didn't want to deal with either.

Dragons had exceptional sight, even in human form, but lately... The light was never strong enough to read the small print on anything. Also, since when was anything "small print"?

It started that day I'd had to turn on every light in my kitchen just so I could barely make out the recipe for the cake I'd been preparing. Don't judge. There wasn't much out there that was more relaxing than getting my bake on, especially after a hard workout.

But then it went from small print in the kitchen to increasing the font size on my computer to roughly double. It was ridiculous to deny reality, so I'd caved and gotten some reading glasses.

A dragon with reading glasses.

Again, depending on their mood, the guys would die of hilarity or think the world was coming to an end.

Not that my hot stalker seemed to mind them. She was once again eyeing me like I was a treat she'd like to lick and suck and—

Fuck. I didn't need a hard-on in the library. There were kids here. I'd get labeled as a perv, banned, and then I wouldn't get to see stalker girl any more.

I returned to my modern myths and legends book. But I couldn't read the words.

My sight hadn't suddenly gotten worse. No, I stopped reading because I was too busy freaking out. Just because I was old as dirt, had lived through more wars than I could count and fought in a good number of them, didn't mean I couldn't get my twelve-year-old-little-boy-freak-out rolling like an actual twelve-year-old.

I knew this about myself. It was why I meditated, worked out regularly, and did some other coping bullshit. Because my brain could occasionally be my enemy.

For the most part, I'd been trying not to think too much about my situation. *Focus on a solution.*

Do some research. Figure out what had happened. Fix it.

An action plan that allowed me to maintain my calm.

In general, my advice to my inner twelve-year-old was to not freak. Because if I did, the next thing I knew, I'd be leaning into Bain and Archer's recommendations of violence, and I wasn't that guy. Not anymore.

I was trying to be all Zen and shit these days.

But... My glasses weren't the only issue. Pretty sure I was losing my close vision because my eyes were *aging*. My eyes shouldn't be aging so quickly, because *I* didn't age that quickly. At least I didn't when I wasn't hexed by some unknown witch with some unknown complaint.

I'd also found a few gray hairs and some creasing around my eyes that hadn't been there before. I might have bought eye cream.

If I was vain, which I wasn't.

Okay, whatever. I bought eye cream.

That would have the guys in stitches, right up until they realized what it meant. I was aging rapidly by dragon standards, which also meant that my ability to heal myself had been damaged or bound along with my dragon.

This no-healing, aging shit was no joke. I'd even considered skipping one of my runs with Chelsea this week, because I'd still been sore from a workout the previous day. But then her sweet brown eyes had persuaded me otherwise. Also, she'd eat half my house if she didn't get enough exercise. Malinois weren't exactly couch potatoes.

But the point was that I'd been sore. I'd taken extra care with cooling out and stretching, and I'd still been noticeably achy. That wasn't normal. Not at all.

And tied up in all that was the reason for my freak-out: Chelsea. The one real concern with this hex was that it would have a negative effect on my dog. My dogs lived long lives. Magically long. It wasn't anything that I overtly did. I was no spell-casting witch. I could throw magical fire, kick some creature ass, and generally hold my own in a fight whether in dragon or human form. Even though it wasn't within my magical abilities to affect the longevity of another being, my pets lived long lives.

Some of my magic rubbing off because of the close contact? Maybe.

This curious effect wasn't limited to dogs. I had a horse once that had lived to be sixty-three and only died because some asshole hit him with an arrow.

(That guy didn't live much longer than my horse.) But this trick I had of imbuing my pets with longevity wasn't something I wanted to risk losing.

And that thought was trying to push my panic button: what if my temporarily diminished capacity meant I wasn't the only one aging?

So far Chelsea hadn't shown any signs of advanced canine age. I was the only one of the two of us to have gray hair overnight. But if I saw any indication that she was, I'd really lose my shit.

And if Chels had her life cut short because of some witch with a grudge, there would be blood.

Stalker girl stopped typing. I shouldn't have noticed. I was busy considering disembowelment of a faceless witch, but she was typing like a journalist on a tight deadline or a highly caffeinated college student who'd waited till the last second to finish her essay—and then just stopped.

The cessation of all that movement was hard to miss.

Probably just as well. I wasn't that disemboweling guy any more. Mostly. Unless someone fucked with my dog.

3

KAYLEE

I was sneaking more than the occasional surreptitious glance at my nerdy hottie. Otherwise I'd never have noticed, but he was sitting at his favorite reading table having a mini-meltdown.

I knew the signs.

I'd been a shy introvert as a kid, raised by a single father who thought that socializing was a healthy, normal way to behave. My dad was all about "normal" behavior. I'd been put in more situations that had stressed me almost beyond my capacity to cope than I liked to remember.

So yeah, I recognized the signs.

He looked like he was about ready to burst from

his skin. Fidgety, jaw clenched, a frantic light in his eyes.

It was my concern for his well-being that led to my downfall. I looked and I let that look linger. And then it happened.

He saw me.

Shit.

He caught me staring. Not that it was probably anything new for him. With a body like that? A smile like that? (Yes, he was smiling at me now, and I couldn't look away.) Definitely this guy was used to being stared at.

He'd probably been an athlete. He had that look. Football? He wasn't quite that beefy, but then not all football players looked like they could eat a small cow and bench-press a larger one. Even so... Maybe basketball or hockey. I'd say a goalie, up until he lost all his chill. He had a massive wingspan, really nice shoulders.

Oh my god, why couldn't I look away?

He was standing up.

Shit. Shit, shit, shit. He was coming this way.

I could feel my face burning.

I might write all the meet-cutes. Really, all of them. I'd written more than thirty romances—or Kitty Sweet had. But since I was Kitty, same difference.

But writing a meet-cute was completely different from *living* it.

Dammit, I was sweating.

Not that I was a virgin. I liked sex. Sex was good.

And that was the thought in my head as nerdy hot guy arrived to stand in front of me: *sex is good.*

He extended his hand. "I'm Dex."

Hell. My hand tentatively made its own way into his. I certainly didn't give it permission. And what was this Dex guy thinking? We made eye contact for maybe point three seconds, and that gave him permission to introduce himself?

There was a flash of surprise on his face before he relinquished my misbehaving appendage. *Bad hand, bad.* He'd probably been grossed out by the dampness. Stupid nerves.

If this was a meet-cute in one of my books, then the hero would be totally into the heroine. He'd be thinking about fucking her against a wall in the bathroom. Or maybe a supply closet. No, he'd be thinking about banging her in the back seat of his sexmobile. No, no...an empty office, after he swept a bunch of books and papers off the desk. He'd fuck her from behind, and smack her ass.

The clearing of my muse's throat intruded into

my dirty imaginings. Rude. Couldn't he wait another few seconds? I could get a (fictional) girl off in less than thirty seconds.

But then I realized I'd let myself be pulled into fantasy—as one did when one was a writer; completely normal; nothing weird to see here—and hadn't introduced myself.

"I'm Kitty, um, Kaylee." I swallowed the tortured groan that was rising to my lips. "I mean, I'm Kaylee. Hi."

My inability to hold a normal conversation with a hot guy was but one way in which my life failed to live up to the fictional lives of my heroines. As much as Dex was indeed a romance hero, as demonstrated by his presence in my work in progress as Drake, I was no heroine.

I was just awkward, weird, quiet me.

"Hi Kitty-Kaylee." *Nooo.* I totally deserved that, but *no.* He ignored my distress or, being a guy, didn't even notice it, and continued, "We both seem to visit the library around the same time, so I thought I'd introduce myself."

I smiled, but it was a weird smile. Kind of strained and lacking any real joy or happiness. I suspected it looked a bit like a grimace. But it was that or actually say something, and speaking seemed ill-advised at the moment. I'd practically outed myself to a stranger. Not many people knew I was Kitty Sweet.

All that previous secrecy with my pen name and with one smile and a handshake, I'd almost spilled all the tea on my pseudonym to a complete stranger. That had never happened before.

Then again, when was the last time a smoking-hot guy approached me and tried engaging me in conversation?

Yeah, that would be never. Because I was weird and quiet and socially awkward.

"So, you seem to be typing a lot. What, are you writing a book or something?" Then he grinned, like, of course I wasn't writing a book.

Except I was. I totally was. And he was the star attraction in all his muscly, nerdy-hot, eyeglass-wearing glory.

And actually, I was kind of annoyed with him. He wasn't a very cooperative hero. I was supposed to be writing some light bondage, mild kink romantic suspense, and it was coming out all dragons and fangs and claws. I didn't write fantasy. Never had, never planned to, and I had good reason for that. But I was desperate. Better fangs and claws than no words at all. And it would be fine. I could deal with a little fictional magic.

Dex looked at me like he was a little amused and a lot confused, which was when I realized that I was glaring at him.

Oops. I grimace-smiled again.

"So, not writing a book."

I skipped over the implied question, because it wasn't really any of his business what I was typing on my computer. But turnabout being fair play and all that, I asked, "What have you been researching?"

And only after I asked did I realize how revealing the question was. Not "reading" but "researching."

The guy had piles of books he scanned each morning. He was obviously researching something. Anyone would know that. Even someone who hadn't been stalking him.

Which I hadn't. At all.

I'd been imagining him naked, but definitely not stalking him.

The grin was back, so he definitely caught my slipup. Dammit. "Myths, legends, magic."

"Sorry?"

"You asked what I was researching. Myths, legends, and magic. Don't suppose you have anything to add on the subject?"

The blood must have rushed somewhere not my head. Or I wasn't breathing normally. Because all of a sudden I was terribly light-headed, and I was still sitting down.

This stranger couldn't possibly know about my problem, no matter how much the inflection in his voice indicated otherwise.

No one knew. No one except my dad and my therapist.

I knew better than to tell anyone. The last time I had, I'd ended up losing my best friend and was laughed at by all the kids at school. Granted, I'd only been eight or nine at the time, but I wasn't so sure adults were all that much kinder.

Besides, I didn't have that problem any more.

Monsters weren't real, and the overactive imagination of my childhood that had tried to convince me they were had faded over time.

Sure, every once in a great while I catch something out of the corner of my eye that couldn't possibly exist, but even my therapist said that was completely normal.

Not exactly the word she'd used, but whatever; the implication had been there. Regular people—the kind who hadn't as a child seen ghosts and gremlins, witches and warlocks, demons and angels—

even normal people caught the occasional glimmer of something unidentifiable in their peripheral vision.

That was me. Completely normal. Seeing completely normal things.

Not a whackadoo with an overactive imagination and a slipping grip on reality.

No one had ever labeled those magical and wondrous things I'd claimed to see as a kid with the frightening "H" word, but as I'd gotten older, I realized that seeing things that weren't really there was literally the definition of an hallucination.

And that was when I'd stopped seeing them.

No more frolicking lizards with sparkly hides or barely visible, delicately translucent wings on the backs of passersby or women with eyes of fire or men with eyes of ice or people who reminded me of animals, as if they hid a creature inside that waited to burst free.

People were just people, and animals, lizard or otherwise, didn't sparkle.

I switched schools and was careful never ever to tell anyone that once upon a time I'd made friends with the dust ball that lived in my house. That he had purple eyes, was named Harry, and loved to eat all the dust he could find and sometimes bits of hair as well.

First, in retrospect, Harry was sort of gross. And second, obviously he'd been a figment of my imagination. So I was a disgusting little kid. That didn't mean I'd been unbalanced. A bit weird, yes. I'd never been normal in the sense that I was like other kids, but there wasn't anything really wrong with me.

And I'd spent the next decade proving it to myself and my poor father, who'd just wanted me to be like all the other children.

My head was between my legs. When did that happen?

And there was a warm hand on my back. A very large, very warm hand that was gently rubbing between my shoulder blades.

I looked up into a gorgeous pair of mossy-green eyes. The glasses were gone. I noticed that he only wore them when he read. Funny, because he looked like he couldn't be more than midthirties at most. I thought people who wore readers were older than me.

This close, I could see that his medium-brown hair was actually more of a chestnut color. There also was a lot of red in that sexy lumberjack beard of his.

The soothing rub on my back stopped, and Dex knelt next to me. He was so close I could smell him. Was that vanilla? And sugar? Did Dex smell like cake? Please, Lord, no. I loved cake. "Go out on a date with me."

"What?" I must have been overcome by the scent of baked goods and delicious man, because I thought Dex just asked me out.

4

DEX

Plot twist: my stalker girl had some magic.

Felt like demon magic, but she wasn't a witch. Not enough magic to be a witch, not if it had taken touch to discern.

I'd guess human and demon parentage, but not quite enough magic to manifest witch powers. Or maybe her magic was suppressed? Hard to say.

What I did know was this.

One, she had magic. I could feel it. I might be broken right now, but I could still feel and see magic. When I held her hand in mine, I could feel the pulse of it inside her.

Two, she was in denial. Her freak-out when I implied she knew something about magic was pretty telling. I encouraged her to put her head between her knees. I'd never seen anyone pass out from a sitting position, but I didn't want today to be the first time.

But the third thing was the most relevant. To me, anyway. I wanted her. Really wanted her. Not like the passing fling with the deli delivery girl or a quick screw in the bathroom with the hot bartender. That had been lust, certainly, but not the same hot want I felt for Kaylee.

I'd been intrigued by her this last week. All the sneaky glances combined with the shyness. The occasional glimpses of her amazing figure hidden beneath the baggy clothing of an octogenarian with a circulation problem. The frantic typing that I was now almost certain was a book. That or a secret plan to take over the world. I was definitely intrigued.

Then I touched her hand, and I went from intrigued to very interested. But *then* I caught her scent. Forget intrigued and interested. I was hungry for her. If she repeated that look from before, the one that said I want to drag you to the farthest corner of the library and suck you off, we'd be headed to the travel section, the possibility of discovery be damned.

But I didn't drag her to the travel section. Or even back to biographies for a quick kiss. I asked her out.

While she was recovering from almost passing out.

Not my finest moment. I lost my head, but who could blame me? She was fuck hot and adorable and she smelled like cuddles and sex. Not actual sex, but like someone I wanted to have sex with. Someone I was a little desperate to have sex with.

Basically, she made me so horny, I lost all my calm.

There wasn't enough meditation to make this burn fade. I was going to have to fuck this lust into oblivion.

"What?" She looked at me with panic is her pretty brown eyes.

Women responded to me in a variety of ways, almost all positive. Panic was new. "A date. You and me."

"Uh, no. Thanks. I mean, no thank you." She blinked at me. "But, ah, it's not you, it's me?" Then she winced and flashed that same smile she'd been sporting since I walked up to her: one part adorable cuteness (she had dimples), two parts fuck-hot woman (her lips had a seductive curve I wanted to bite), and three parts completely uncomfortable (she had absolutely no fucking clue how gorgeous she was).

I couldn't help it. I laughed. She was so adorably flustered—over being asked out. Hot women didn't get flustered from being hit on. Kitty-Kaylee was a gem.

A gem who'd definitely just turned me down. But that wasn't a "no" from a woman who wasn't interested. That was a "no" from a woman who'd been asked out by an utter ass while she'd been in the midst of an anxiety attack.

Not to say she *was* interested. That was still an unknown.

I stood up and moved far enough away that I wasn't looming. "Fair enough. And apologies, I shouldn't have just asked like that."

"No?" She didn't seem entirely certain.

"No. Promise you won't hold it against me?" Then I flashed her a smile that had served me well for centuries.

It didn't fail me.

"Ah, okay?" She sat all the way up.

"So you won't avoid the library?"

She took a slow breath, and I could see her chest expanding. Using breath to mitigate anxiety, a sign that she was in familiar territory with that panic attack. After two breaths, she said, "No, I won't avoid the library. I like writing here."

Good enough for now. I had the beginnings of a plan, and her continued presence here was pivotal. I flashed her what I hoped was a nonthreatening smile and took another quarter step back.

She bit her lip, then said, "I'm sort of new. To Austin. To the neighborhood. My house is within walking distance, and I really do love writing here."

Her eyes opened wide, as if she was surprised that she'd revealed that information. It was more than I'd hoped for. And it also gave me another prong for that plan I was hatching.

"Excellent. It was nice to meet you, Kaylee." I omitted the Kitty this time. It had flustered her before, and I didn't need my skittish girl any more rattled than she already was. For the plan to work, she had to keep up her morning library habit.

"Um, yeah. Same. Nice to meet you, Drake. I mean, Dex." She blushed a pretty rose color, clearly embarrassed to have fumbled my name.

What an interesting slip to make. Unless she was a particular fan of the musician and happened to have him on her mind, I'd hazard a guess that her subconscious caught my true nature.

Because what was Drake but another name for dragon?

5

KAYLEE

That laugh. I wanted to melt and not in embarrassment. He wasn't laughing at me. No, that was a warm, self-deprecating, sexy-as-hell laugh.

He was laughing at himself—after asking me out. That really should be offensive.

And yet...it wasn't. Because I was pretty sure he was finding humor in his poor choice of timing, not the fact of inviting me on a date.

Maybe, because I was half in love and totally in lust with the guy, I was attributing motivations to him that weren't real.

Or maybe he was a decent guy with a good sense of humor?

I tilted my head as I watched his ass. The

distance from my corner to the table he'd claimed was only a few feet, sadly, because that was one fine ass. Nice full globes, like he did plenty of squats at the gym. Or maybe he really was a hockey player. Hockey butt was real. I was a romance writer. I knew these things.

I sighed, then turned my attention to packing up before he spotted me ogling him. I wouldn't get any more words this morning. My head was too full of that beyond-awkward exchange I'd just shared with Drake—dammit! Dex—leaving no room for story shenanigans to unfold.

And we were definitely in the shenanigans part of the book. The were-dragon Drake had just claimed his sexy, badass mate (who happened to have my hair and eyes), and they were going to get it on in Drake's lair.

Not really sure what my readers would think about this one. It wasn't exactly my normal fare. But dammit, Drake was all I could write the last week. I probably wouldn't even publish this one. Just add it to the drawer of stories that would never see the light of day. But I knew that I had to get it done if I wanted to move onto a more appropriate story. Drake was my springboard to my next romantic suspense hero.

Time to walk home, make myself an early lunch, and not think about sexy, bearded, lumberjack, hockey-butt men who wore reading glasses and smelled like an upscale cake shop—the kind that used real butter, expensive vanilla, and where everything looked so beautiful you almost didn't want to eat it.

Dammit. I was comparing Drake—Dex!—to a freaking cake shop. Dex wasn't cake, much as I'd like to eat him up.

That man. This was his fault. He'd insinuated himself into my book, my head. Hell, next thing I knew I'd be dreaming about him.

The last few days I'd been thankful for the words; I still was. I'd been telling myself vaguely that I'd fix all the dragon nonsense in editing. Wings and claws could totally be a badge and a gun. Not really, but sometimes these lies needed to be told. Dragon words were far better than no words and the dread that consumed me when I was supposed to be writing and wasn't. And I really did think that releasing the story onto the page was getting me past my block.

But now I had a problem. Now the nerdy-hot guy who'd been a fictional dragon helping me with a little writer's block had turned into a real man. The kind who was hitting on me.

Danger, danger, danger.

I needed a reality check, and definitely no more intimate chats with Dex. Guys like that didn't date women like me.

Fuck? Yes, probably. I'd bet that if Dex notched his bedpost, it would be kindling. I was just fine as a one night stand. I knew from experience that a lot of guys weren't super picky about who they screwed, but they were much pickier about anything more. I was fine for a little fun, but too weird to date. Fuck that.

By the time I arrived home, I'd spun myself into a tizzy. I needed the words, but the words were all about Drake. Drake was actually Dex, and now he was trying to invade my real, nonfictional life.

Warnings kept flashing in my head, much like the back-up signal on a forklift. *Worlds colliding. Imminent danger. Worlds colliding. Imminent danger.*

There was a simple answer: avoid the library.

Yeah, I wasn't going to do that. I sort of promised I'd be back. Also... I wanted to go back. Staring at all that fineness was helping me finish a book, even if it wasn't the book I'd intended to write.

I walked into my house feeling like my brain was

overcooked. I was exhausted from the minor panic attack I'd had. Also from my exchange with Drake—dammit, Dex!—because that man was exhausting. But mostly it was the dizzying back and forth of my situation that had worn me out.

To finish the book I had to write Drake. To write Drake, I basically needed Dex. To expose myself to Dex was to put myself near the fires of an IRL relationship. The only kind of IRL relationship Dex could possibly want was the one night stand variety, and I wasn't a one night stand kind of girl. Not when it came to someone like Dex. I'd catch feelings.

So I should avoid him.

But I couldn't, because I wanted, maybe needed, to finish Drake's book. To write Drake, I basically needed Dex. And so on, into infinity.

Yep, dizzying. The loop de loop of it all was exhausting.

I was taking a nap.

I SETTLED over his warm body, my thighs straddling his hips, my hands on his gorgeous muscled shoulders.

Hard, flat male nipples pebbled against my

tongue. I licked and sucked, loving the taste of him. Vanilla. A touch of sweetness. And something elusive, indescribable, male.

I wiggled, settling my needy center over his hardness, then I began to move, riding his length without letting him penetrate me. I was in control as I sucked and bit his chest and came close to getting myself off on his dick.

He smacked my ass. "Enough."

That was it, just one word and the sharp sting of pain, and I was at his mercy. I was already drenched, ready for him. But the slap and then hearing the deep timbre of his lust-roughened voice—I went from ready to desperate.

He flipped me over and kissed me. He tasted of vanilla, of cake, of him. He tasted like...magic. My mind stuttered over the forbidden word.

He entered me. Hot and hard, stretching me, bottoming out with one deep thrust. I forgot all about taboo words, lost it in a bigger moment. A better one, far from the past.

Breath coming in gasps as my body adjusted, I gave myself over to him. He took that surrender as his due, growling as he thrust inside me.

I could only cling to him as he—

A loud pounding knock at my door jerked me awake.

"Dammit, Dex!" Not that I thought nerdy-hot library guy had followed me home and interrupted my dream. No, I knew who was at my door. That knock was uniquely Mathilde's. My elderly neighbor, four doors down and around the corner, loved to swing by around lunchtime for a "chat." That was her code word for lunch. She knew if I was making lunch, I'd invite her to join me.

Mathilde was a terrible cook. If I didn't feed her, I was sure she'd live on canned soup and sandwiches with the occasional salad thrown in. I really don't know how she managed before I moved to the neighborhood a few months ago. From what I could tell, she had no family. Though she was cagey about the topic, so I could be wrong.

I was pissed at Dex, because he was creeping into my dreams. Mathilde was expected and welcome, if maybe a little early.

Bad enough I had to deal with Dex invading my story. That was a necessary evil. Obviously. If my merry-go-round of indecision had revealed anything, it was that I'd be stuck in an infinity loop of denial and desire if I didn't just woman up and admit I needed Dex to finish my book and I was finishing the damn book. But now he was in my dreams, as well? Not cool, Dex. Not cool, at all.

I scrambled out of bed, called out, "Coming!" then stopped in my bathroom to splash water on my face. The last thing I needed was Mathilde guessing that she'd interrupted me in the midst of a sex dream, and my flushed face was a dead giveaway.

The thought of discovery was terrifying. She'd already tried to set me up with the mailman, the pizza guy, and the man who sprayed her house for bugs. She didn't get out much, but she sure took advantage of any encounter with men under the age of fifty to pimp me out.

It was sweet and annoying. Mostly annoying. But if she got wind that there was a man in my life who inspired naughty dreams, hell, there would be no stopping her.

I stood in front of the door thinking the opposite of lustful thoughts, took a breath, then swung it open.

She gave me a critical look, then shook her head. "I have a man for you."

Eighty-five if she was a day, Mathilde was that woman all women aspired to be as they aged: fit, active, sharp as a blood-drawing tack, and beautiful.

I'd heard the saying "good bones" but hadn't

truly understood until I'd met Mathilde. She was glamorous, and if a woman could look glamorous wearing the twin of my oatmeal-colored fluffy cardigan (a birthday gift from me; it even had pockets!), well, that meant that she was basically a movie star or a model.

I leaned on the doorframe, barring entry. "And if I don't want to go out with your plumber?"

She frowned. "He's not my plumber. He's a neighbor."

I lifted my eyebrows. That was even worse. If I did actually go on a date with this one and it didn't end well (spoiler: my dates *never* ended well), the chances were much higher than average that I'd run into him again. "No way."

"Why not?" She pulled her cardigan tighter around her body, hinting that she was getting cold.

I groaned, but relented and stepped to the side, inviting her in. We'd had a cool front, making the fall air a little chillier than normal. "You know why not."

"You mean Chester? I can't believe you agreed to go out with him."

I stared at her back as she made her way to my kitchen. "You set me up with him!"

Her thin shoulders lifted in a shrug, but she didn't pause in her journey to my fridge. "Yes, but I expected you to say no like you did with all the others. Those men were just practice."

Trailing behind her, I tried to figure out what exactly that meant. I'd only gone out with the one and apparently wasn't supposed to have said yes, so... "How were they practice?"

She opened the fridge door, and I waited to see what kind of day this was: soda water or mimosas. She pulled a bottle of bubbly from the depths. When she turned to hand the bottle over, she smiled. "I was practicing. I had to figure out what buttons to push to get you to say yes, didn't I?"

As I took the bottle from her, I resisted returning her smile. Even though I was annoyed, I knew she was trying to help. Regardless, the meddling wench needed *no* encouragement.

Sometimes I wondered if Mathilde was a peek into what it would have been like to have a mother growing up. Mine hadn't bothered to stick around, but I'd seen how other people's relationships with their moms worked. This determination to see me paired off reminded me of that.

Dad seemed just fine with me staying single forever. I had my own theories of why that might be true, none of which were particularly flattering to either of us.

I turned my attention to popping the cork. It really was a mimosa kind of day.

"You need to say yes to this one."

I swallowed a sigh. "Because he's a better match for me than Chester?"

She waved a dismissive hand. "Forget Chester. That was a mistake, and I apologize. If I'd known you'd cave so quickly, I'd have just asked you to go out with the first two as practice."

Pretty sure Mathilde was missing the point, but since we were about to split a bottle of bubbly, I might as well wait until she was a little tipsy before trying to untwist her convoluted logic.

I poured grocery store sparkling wine into the two crystal flutes Mathilde had retrieved from my china cabinet. A gift from her, naturally. I wasn't really a crystal sort of girl. The rest of my china cabinet was filled with glass vases, everyday teapots, and a few pretty plates that didn't have any real monetary value but made me happy.

When she made a humming noise, I added a bit more. Mathilde was quite particular about her orange-juice-to-bubbly ratios. But then I noticed she hadn't fetched the OJ.

"We're toasting." She looked pointedly at the glasses, so I filled them all the way.

I didn't want to ask why exactly we were raising our glasses, because I suspected I knew. I probably couldn't wiggle my way out of a coffee date with this neighbor guy if she was this excited about it. I didn't want to hurt her feelings.

Which was how I ended up going out with pest guy Chester. Nice enough fellow, but he was forty-nine to my thirty-one, didn't read books, thought romance novels were "silly," and didn't have the sense to backtrack from that stance when I disclosed I wrote them for a living. Instead, the man had questioned whether that was smart financially, implying that I must either be on the brink of poverty or have some support from a male relative. It had been a short date.

"I cast a love spell, and it's landed on the neighbor. He's the one. You have to go out with him." Her eyes sparkled with excitement.

I hadn't seen that one coming. Not at all. Not in a million years.

A love spell?

"Close your mouth, darling. You'll catch flies."

I snapped my mouth shut.

Mathilde lifted her glass, then looked pointedly at the one in my hand that I'd forgotten about. I raised mine, and we clinked.

I'd just toasted a love spell.

"To love!" And for just a split second, I thought I saw an actual sparkle in her eyes. The glowy kind that I used to see when I was a child.

Given my fraught history with all things fantastical—magic and spells most definitely included—I couldn't quite manage to get any words out. Especially in the face of that glow I hadn't seen, because it hadn't been there.

I drank the glass of bubbly in its entirety. Then I poured another.

6

DEX

I had a plan. It wasn't fully fleshed out, but it was a start. I had an end goal, a few steps worked out, and the rest I'd develop as I moved forward. Best to be flexible in these situations.

Kaylee was shy, so she needed a little time to acclimate to new people. She needed some time to get used to the idea of me. A me who knew she existed and was interested, as opposed to the stranger she'd been eying on the sly.

No problem. I could become a quiet, unobtrusive fixture. For now.

So I worked out, ran with Chelsea, managed my portfolio, and generally kept to my regular routine—

which now included a daily early-morning trip to the library.

There was research and reading—I was still broken, and I still needed to be fixed—but that wasn't my primary focus. I was mostly there so I could tell Kaylee "hello," and then leave her in peace to work and stalk me all she liked.

I accompanied that greeting with a friendly smile that wasn't too warm, so I didn't scare her off.

When she left, she made a point of smiling in my direction, and I waved goodbye. It was all very laid back. No pressure.

Three days of that, and I decided it was time to move to the next stage, especially since she'd gotten so wary of being caught checking me out that she'd almost stopped ogling me.

That wasn't good. The only thing I had going for me at this point was whatever attraction she had for me. She could hardly get to know me if she wouldn't go out with me.

So after the third morning, I decided it was time for the secondary prong in my plan. Honestly, it was a long shot as an actual part of my plan, but something told me it was a good idea in general. Good for a shy, quiet woman who'd just moved to the area.

Taylor, Bain's mate, lived just a few miles down

the road. Her neighborhood and mine practically ran into each other. Pretty sure that meant my library was her library.

Which meant that Kaylee's library was Taylor's library.

Taylor had mentioned she was interested in making new friends—good choice; her last few girlfriends had been questionable in the kindness department—and again, Kaylee was new to the area. I had no clue whether Kaylee was interested in meeting new people, but I knew it was important to have amazing friends and Taylor was good people.

I wasn't planning anything underhanded. I was going to be—mostly—transparent.

I knew Bain would be at Taylor's for lunch, because they always ate together. Lunch *and* dinner. Hell, probably breakfast, as well, considering they were shacking up most nights. Those two were ridiculous.

I texted ahead of time, because the last thing I wanted to do was interrupt them boning. I really liked Taylor, and I didn't want to see her freshly fucked look. I didn't need to know that sort of shit about her.

Also, I sometimes got the impression Taylor was

a little suspicious of me. Turning up unannounced on her doorstep might not go over well.

When I asked Bain why she occasionally eyeballed me like I might steal her lunch money, he mentioned something about me violating her purse.

I couldn't believe she remembered that night. She'd been ridiculously drunk. The only reason I'd "violated" her purse was to find her car keys so I could deliver her car to her house. She sure as hell hadn't been in a state to drive.

But then she'd also made Bain a little nuts that night by mentioning that I had a nice laugh.

So, yeah, it could go either way with Taylor. I had a nice laugh, and I violated purses.

"Am I feeding you?" she asked after opening her pink door. It was a nice enough little bungalow, but a pink door? And not a pink that was trying for red and failing. This door was decidedly pastel pink.

Bain had three other places in or near town, all bigger, and none with a pink door. Why they always landed at Taylor's place was a mystery.

"Good to see you, too." I flashed her my nice-guy smile.

She narrowed her eyes. "I hid my purse, just in case." I can only imagine the look on my face, because she chuckled. "Gotcha. But no, really, am I feeding you? You're welcome, I just need to make more pasta if you're planning to eat with us. I know how much y'all can put away."

Y'all being shifters or Bain's friends, I wasn't sure. Bain, Archer, and I all ate like men who stayed active...and occasionally flew around in the sky as dragons burning thousands of calories at the drop of a hat. Flight was predominantly achieved through magical means, but wielding that much magic cost energy.

Her foot tapped as she waited for my reply. For such a tiny thing, she was a ball of fire.

"For what's it worth, if I knew you were going to give me hell over it, I'd have made Bain dig out your keys."

She put her hands on her hips. "Bain would have known better."

What was her weird obsession with her purse's privacy? Like it was its own person or something. But then, Taylor was kind of an oddball. Thankfully, she was odd in all the ways that Bain was, or at least in compatible ways, because those two couldn't be better mated.

I'd love to find that. Someday. Everyone knew dragon mates were few and far between. That soul-deep connection eluded most of us. A simple fact of life. When Bain and Taylor had first fallen for each other, I'd thought: *Maybe me*? Especially when I heard a rumor about another dragon being mated out west. But then reality set in. I wouldn't make the mistake Bain had. He'd believed himself mated before Taylor. Delusional on his part, since his ex had been as far from his soul mate as possible, but he'd convinced himself because he'd wanted it so much.

I let Taylor keep the illusion that Bain would have respected the sanctity of her purse, and kept my mouth shut on the topic. "Don't go to any trouble on my account. Unlike your grumpy bastard boyfriend, I can feed myself."

Bain appeared behind her and with his hand on her back, hustled her none too subtly back into the house out of the fall draft. I was still standing on the doorstep, and that was just how Bain wanted it. "I can cook just fine, asshole. We trade who cooks, not that it's any business of yours. Why are you here?"

"Good to see you, too, buddy." When he just lifted his eyebrows, I said, "I have a favor to ask."

The scowl was back.

He glanced over his shoulder then lowered his voice. "You know how Taylor is. The company she works for gives her an hour for lunch, and she takes exactly sixty minutes. You're wasting precious time here, *buddy*." Then he added a nice glower for good measure.

Bain was a big guy, but he was loyal as hell when it came to his friends. Archer might kick my ass for screwing up his booty call, but Bain? No way.

Then my loyal friend growled, and I realized that Bain might feel differently about Taylor, his *mate*, than some booty call.

Something in my expression must have given me away, because he stopped with the growly bullshit and sighed, then motioned me inside.

It was hard not to be envious of the guy. He'd scored the golden ticket. Landed the dream of a life-time. Of course I was envious. That didn't mean I begrudged him finding his mate. Just that I wanted what he had. And he had to know that, whether it was written across my face or not.

Fuck fate and our cursed race. I was living my life, and right now, I had a sweet, shy, gorgeous stalker in my sights. So what if she wasn't the love of my life, my soul mate, the only one I could have chil-dren with. She was intriguing, and that was a start—to something, even if that something was less than a mate bond. I'd learned to live with compromise a very long time ago.

"What's this favor?" he asked as he headed toward the delicious scents of garlic and Italian seasonings.

"Ah, it's not a favor from you."

He turned and leveled me a withering stare.

I rolled my eyes. "Try that shit with the rat-shifters. Not gonna work on me. Besides," I grinned at Taylor, who had paused in dishing out salad to see what we were arguing about. "Taylor's an adult. She can make her own decisions."

"Taylor is an adult," she agreed, "but she's also crazy about the grumpy guy behind you. Fair warning, I'm on his side. Always."

"It's not that kind of favor. There aren't any sides. Actually, I think it'll be mutually beneficial." Before Bain could take that the wrong way, I said, "You mentioned you were interested in making some new friends. How's that going?"

"Sounds good in theory, harder to execute. Especially since I'm working from home these days and have less time in general." She shot a lovey look at Bain, so there was no doubting her meaning.

"But you wouldn't mind extending a hand in friendship to another lovely lady who's new to the area?"

The soft melting look vanished. "Dex, what shenanigans are you getting up to?"

"No shenanigans. I need you to make friends with a girl at the library."

Taylor looked at me as if I'd asked her to set foot outside her home in curlers. In Taylor's world, that was a gross breach of behavior.

"I am not sex matchmaking for you." She scowled. It was kind of cute, sort of a mini, adorable version of Bain's expression. The two of them had definitely been spending too much time together.

"I don't know what that is." I looked to Bain for a translation.

"Pimping," he explained succinctly.

Since Taylor's cheeks immediately turned pink and she didn't deny it, I guessed he was right.

"I don't need a pimp." As if getting tail was a problem for me. I refrained from saying as much, though. "She's new in town, and she doesn't have any friends. You're a nice woman and she's a nice woman..."

"Wait a second." Taylor squinted at me, as if trying to pull forth any hidden ill intent with the power of her mind. She was a psychic, but not a powerful one. And they couldn't read minds anyway.

I waited.

Finally, her expression cleared of suspicion. "Two questions. Is she judgmental?"

"Ah, I don't think so?"

Taylor turned pinker. "You don't think so? How well do you know this woman?"

"Not well, but I think she's shy, and she turned me down when I asked her out. I think she's—"

"Nope. No. Uh-uh." Eyes narrowed to slits, she said, "Do we need to have the talk, Dex? Because I am so ready for that talk. No means no."

"It wasn't like that."

"It never is," she murmured.

"Look, she's been kind of stalking me at the library. I went a few mornings in a row, then she showed up, and she started, you know, checking me out. She's been back every morning since, and I swear to you, she is spending just as much time looking at me as she is writing."

"Huh."

"Just say no, hon." Bain punctuated that comment with a pointed look at the clock.

"Just because you don't want to miss any lunches." She wagged a finger at him, like he was a naughty schoolboy. Ugh, yeah, I didn't need that visual.

"No, I do not. I think you should quit. Start your

own business. The distillery will be your first client. Then you can take long lunches and it won't be a problem when annoying friends swing by with annoying requests."

"Shush. We've already talked about this. Besides, no one ever swings by at lunch but you." Taylor turned to me with a wry look. "And Dex when he wants to beg a favor. Why do you want to get to know this woman so badly?"

"She's interesting." And really attractive in a slouchy-sweater, messy-hair kind of way. That way that shines through bad fashion choices.

"How do you know that? You don't know her."

Bain's grin was evil. "She has a point. Just admit it. She's fuck hot and you want some of that, and you're using my mate to sex matchmake."

And now the guy was just trying to push my buttons. And Taylor's.

Ignoring Bain's idiocy, I replied to Taylor. "She's interesting enough that I want to get to know her better. And she's shown signs that she's interested, but she's shy."

Good grief. What was with the grilling? A guy asks for a little help, thereby helping not just himself, but also his friend's mate—she said she wanted to make new friends—and this was what I got? Okay, that was sort of bullshit, but still, Taylor could do me a solid.

"Okay, so she's pretty," Taylor said.

"Fuck hot," Bain corrected.

Taylor just pointed her finger at him, and he snapped his mouth shut. Turning to me, she said, "Let me guess, she's interesting *because* she said no."

"No." And I meant it.

"Then why? Why her?" Taylor insisted.

And because she looked truly curious, I gave it some thought.

But... "I don't know, okay? I don't know. I just want a chance at a date. A real chance. A real date. I want to get to know her."

She considered my reply, inadequate as it was, then said, "Okay. I'll do it."

"Wait, what?" The grin that had been on Bain's face disappeared. "You'll do it? What about sex matchmaking?"

"You, sit." Taylor pointed at Bain then one of the chairs at the table. And funny enough, he did.

"You," she pointed at me, "with me."

Then she walked to the front door. Before she opened it, she hollered over her shoulder, "No eaves-dropping, you big scaly beast."

I barked out a laugh. I couldn't help it. Their relationship was just so...them.

She grinned, then opened the front door. "The porch is better. Less temptation to sneak into our conversation with that freakishly good hearing of his."

I stepped out onto her front porch. It looked like she spent very little time gardening, and yet the view onto her front lawn was so very Taylor: charming with its scattered herbs and flowers, whimsical.

My heart warmed that my friend had found Taylor.

Emotion bubbled up, and I couldn't keep it inside. "Thank you."

She shrugged. "You're not wrong. I really do want to make some new friends, and while I have my doubts that some woman you think is stalking you is a great choice—weirder things have happened to me."

"Not what I meant. You're perfect." When her eyes got big, I chuckled. "For Bain. Not that I wish such a terrible experience on you, but if you'd known his ex—"

She held up her hand. "Yeah. I might not have met her, but I've seen some of the mess she left behind." She smiled sweetly. "But he's good now. We're good."

I wondered that they hadn't formalized their relationship. Taylor seemed the marrying kind. Bain wouldn't care one way or another. There was nothing more binding for a dragon than being mated. But Taylor? I'd have thought she'd want the fancy dress, the ceremony, and a big-ass party with an unending supply of McBain's whiskey. Then again, not my business.

"I know I called her a stalker, but Kaylee's not really like that. She's just shy and interested." Taylor's skeptical glance prompted me to defend myself. "I'm okay at reading people. Women. Their interest."

She chuckled. "You're a mess. And that, Dex, is why I'm doing this." She patted my arm.

I wasn't sure how to interpret that. Without Bain as a translator, it was hard to say. Could mean I was generally a mess, and she thought I needed all the help I could get. Could also mean she thought I was making a fool of myself over this woman, and she was down for spectating as I crashed and burned.

"I'm really not just using you as a pimp. You do know that I'm perfectly capable of getting my own dates." Since I was literally asking the woman to help me get a date, I quickly qualified, "*Those* kind of dates."

She started to laugh, turned quite pink, and then doubled over chuckling. When she finally got her hilarity under control, she said, "Good Lord above, this is going to be entertaining."

"Glad to be at your service."

She patted my arm. "Tell me when I need to go and who I'm looking for."

I described Kaylee's chocolate-and-honey hair, her purple laptop, and her grandma sweater, the three things that would make her most easily identifiable to a stranger.

Taylor bit her lip and gave me a funny look, then she smiled and said, "Consider it done."

7

KAYLEE

After drinking half a bottle of sparkling wine, I'd firmly told Mathilde that I wasn't meeting her neighbor. *Our* neighbor.

The following day, I'd opted for a lentil casserole. It was cheesy, but otherwise quite healthy. Mathilde had already told me she didn't have any cholesterol concerns, so I made this dish once a week to share with her.

Over lunch, I explained, "I don't believe in magic."

With a knowing look, she said, "I assumed as much."

"And even if I did, you can't make someone fall in

love. Maybe you could make them *think* they have...
I mean, if I believed in that stuff. But I don't."

"Well, for argument's sake, let's say magic exists.
You'd be exactly right. Magic can only create an illusion of love, not the real deal. That's not what a love
spell does, darling."

I blinked at the intensity in her hazel eyes. She
believed every word. It had been drummed into me
that I shouldn't indulge such fantasies. For my own
good. What about for the good of others?

Was it really fair to attack Mathilde's beliefs? It
wasn't as if she saw things that weren't there. *She*
didn't have a pet named Harry who ate dust and hair.

"Fine. Just so we're clear, I don't believe in spells,
but I respect the fact that you believe in them." Wow,
that came out way more condescending than I'd
intended. I started to apologize, but Mathilde
stopped me with a blinding smile.

She looked like a movie star when she did that. It
was a little terrifying.

She could probably get away with murder if she
only flashed the police that smile—even if she was
holding the bloody knife in her hand and standing
over the corpse. Sheesh.

"I completely understand, and I won't take

offense. You have your baggage, darling, and I have mine. Who am I to rewrite your history?"

"Uh, okay?" I didn't entirely understand what she was getting at. We were talking about philosophical and religious differences here, not baggage. I thought, anyway.

"But just so you know, a love spell isn't meant to be an active sort of spell. It's a bit like that funny mechanical voice that tells you when to turn and when you've arrived at your destination."

I set my fork down. I didn't want that last bite anyway. Too much cheese. "You're saying a love spell is like GPS navigation?"

"Yes! That funny little woman who tells me to turn left after I've passed the road I'm supposed to turn left on." Mathilde leaned forward. "My love spell is much more helpful than that. More accurate, for sure. Love is my 'thing,' as you young people say. My specialty."

Love spells were GPS nav and Mathilde, my octogenarian movie-star neighbor, had a specialty and it was love.

I sat back in my chair. "How long have you been coming to lunches here?"

She grinned, as if she knew where this was

headed. She should. "Three and a half months. Just a few days shy of your move-in date."

"Are you really a terrible cook?"

"Oh, darling, terrible."

"So you didn't make that up, because you met me and thought what a sad little single lady I was and that you could fix it?"

She leaned forward, all seriousness now. "Not a bit of it. I'm a terrible cook, and I make you invite me over for lunch because I think we're both just a little bit lonely. I enjoy your company. So much, Kaylee. I truly do."

My eyes were getting a bit wet, because I really enjoyed her company as well. She was my very best friend in Austin.

She patted my knee and then grinned. "The love spell was just a bonus. It's been so long since I'd done one, and I did wonder how someone as lovely as you could possibly still be single, especially when you don't seem averse to dating." She pursed her lips. "Not entirely averse."

I swallowed a laugh, but couldn't help a broad smile. I loved that she cared, whatever weird ways she chose to demonstrate her affection. Maybe that's why we got along so well: deep down, we were both complete weirdos.

"So long as your heart's in the right place, I guess you can love spell away."

"Well, it was a tiny bit more difficult than I'd realized, it being so long since I gave it a whack. I had to dust off my skills, look a few things up... But that's neither here nor there, because I won't need to do another. As the mechanical voice lady in the car says: you have arrived!"

Oh, my. "The neighbor."

"Yes!"

She was much, much too excited about this guy.

My reluctance being no secret—hell, I probably looked like I'd just sucked a lemon—she decided that persuasion was the name of the game. She started to tick off this nameless man's attributes in her pursuit of what she believed to be my blissful happily-ever-after. "He's attractive. He has stable income. He has lovely taste. His house is quite nice. It's the one—"

"Stop. No identifying details. I can't handle it." The disappointed look on her face prompted me to add, "Yet. Give me a little time to acclimate to the idea."

Lots of time. I could run into this guy at the corner market, the local coffee shop... the library. Awkward to the nth degree.

"Hmph. Not sure what needs acclimating, but all right, no details. Extremely attractive, financially self-sufficient, kind eyes, nice laugh, tall, lots of muscles." She brightened at the thought of his muscles. "Oh, you might see him when he, ah...with his..., never mind. No identifying details."

I raised my eyebrows. "With his extremely fit and attractive girlfriend?"

She made a dismissive noise. "No. Of course not. He's single. He's waiting for *you*. That's how a love spell works. It finds two halves of a whole. He can't be your other half if he's someone else's other half."

She said this as if divorce, adultery, and cheating in general were nonexistent. What a happy place to live, fantasy though it was. My father had married a woman—a lovely, pretty, kind woman—who was on her third marriage with my dad, and Jessica was in her early forties. Her first husband had been a serial cheater and the second had dumped her for a younger model. I'd bet Jessica would have something to say about Mathilde's nonsense.

Then again, Dad and Jessica seemed to be pretty happy.

Mathilde was waiting for some sort of reply, so I tackled the obvious flaw. "And this magical other half of me just so happens to live in my neighborhood."

She pressed her lips together.

"Go on. Say it." There was more woo-woo to come, I had no doubt. My favorite person in Austin had fessed up to casting a love spell. Pretty sure there was more woo-woo. I could deal. At least I wasn't getting all light-headed and weird like I had in the library with Dex.

"Well, since you asked. Why this neighborhood? Why this house? Why Austin?"

The last one was easy enough. "I needed a change. Besides, have you been to Houston? The weather, the traffic." My dad.

I'd definitely needed some space from my dad.

And his new wife. Jessica was great for my dad, but she'd started to insert herself into my life, and I wasn't really up for that. Maybe I was the daughter she'd always wished she'd had? No idea, but Dad hadn't told Jessica about my troubles as a kid. It was awkward. She wanted to get to know me, and I couldn't share one of the biggest hurdles in my life. Also, I was never going to be besties with my dad's significant other. That was just... No.

Dad had not been happy about my move. But since he wasn't the boss of me and hadn't been for well over a decade, I moved to Austin despite his protests.

It was like he didn't trust me to keep it together in his absence. Like I was this fragile creature on the brink of... Honestly, I didn't know what. He'd reassured me he wasn't concerned for my sanity, and I believed him—mostly. He just kept saying that he wanted me to be happy. That it was really important to him that I was happy.

Like a normal dad would do.

I believed him, and yet, if that was the primary concern for me, then wouldn't he be happy to see me move to a new city I was excited about?

"Baggage, am I right?" I returned to the present to find Mathilde smiling gently.

"Okay, yeah. There's some baggage," I agreed. "All the more reason for me to pass on meeting this neighbor guy, who, by the way, was not the reason I chose this house. I love this house."

It was a crazy-cute little nineteen twenties craftsman. Almost entirely white, inside and out, which left me so much room for all the colorful things. A deep purple velvet sofa. A pink shower curtain. A sage green and purple velvet duvet with bedroom furniture to match. Mint green kitchen appliances.

Better yet, a porch just big enough for a table and

two chairs, and a detached "man cave" that I'd turned into my writing space.

My home was my happy place.

Mathilde pushed her empty plate away so there was room for her to rest her elbows on the table. "I think it's a bad idea to put off meeting him."

The hole in her logic was there to be poked, so I did. "But if your love spell says he's my one true love, then it doesn't really matter if I meet him now or later, because we're destined for one another."

"Oh, no. That's not how it works at all, darling." And for the first time, there was a hint of concern in her eyes. "The spell does the finding, the rest is on you. And him."

Of course it was. Even magical love wasn't out to give me an easy happy ending.

Hard pass. I could find my own difficult endings, thank you very much.

And this was why I loved writing. Real life was a downer. Fiction was where all the fun stuff happened.

8

KAYLEE

Dex didn't bother showing up at the library.

Stop, rewind that thought.

For a woman who'd had a good bit of therapy, that was some problematic thinking happening there. Dex wasn't at the library today, for some reason that was unknown to me and might have nothing whatsoever to do with me.

He'd asked me out four days ago, and he'd been perfectly normal since then: greeting me daily, reading books...not asking me out again.

Maybe he'd finished his research yesterday. Maybe yesterday had been his last day at the library.

I hoped not, because... My book, of course. Because of my book.

The words didn't dry up. I could still see Dex in my head. Who could forget that face? The beard that added character rather than hiding his features, those sexy green eyes peering over his glasses. His smile. His devastating smile.

But without his presence, I wasn't as focused.

Utterly bizarre. With as many covert glances as I sent his way, I'd have thought his absence would increase my productivity. Whether it was my efforts to look industrious (and therefore not like a stalker) or that the real-life version of Dex was just that inspiring, I didn't know.

"You're not quite as he described you." The words penetrated the fog of my straying thoughts, and I realized a woman was standing near, watching me type.

Actually, watching me *not* type.

She wasn't hovering, and a quick glance at my screen assured me she couldn't see anything that would give me away. Or rather, that would give away Kitty Sweet.

Hold on a sec, she'd been *looking for me*? "I'm sorry?"

"Dex. He said I'd recognize you by the speed of your rapidly moving fingers. Said you typed like a hacker on a caffeine high."

I started to grin at the analogy—because I was a little intense when I was in the zone—then realized Dex had sent a blonde bombshell babe to stalk me.

What the hell?

"He's not usually a complete nut, so I figured I had to meet you." With a self-deprecating smile, she said, "This is supposed to be like some kind of play date for grown-ups."

Given what I'd been writing when the bubbly blonde appeared—or shortly before she appeared, before I got lost in thoughts of Dex and his devastating smile—it wasn't so odd that I went dirty with that play date comment.

She held up a finger. "Whatever you're thinking, I didn't mean *that*."

I blinked. Who was this woman?

She was like a mind reader, because she held out her hand and smiled. "I'm Taylor, Bain's...ah, girlfriend." When I just blinked, she added, "Dex's friend Bain."

I shook her hand. "You're Dex's friend's girlfriend."

She smiled brightly, as if I'd just grasped a complex concept. "That's right."

A covert scan of the immediate area revealed no

lurking people with cameras. "And why are you here?"

"Partly because Dex is an idiot. Don't frown, the man tried to set up two grown women on a play date. He's an idiot. But mostly because I was curious. Also, he wasn't wrong about me wanting to meet more people. I work from home." She assumed a cute expression of consternation.

Everything this woman did was cute. Except for filling out her dress. She wore the most adorable fit-and-flare dress, retro fifties and not at all something I could carry off. With her curves, she made it look like something a pinup girl would wear. No, not so blatant. A movie star. Or a really elegant nineteen fifties housewife throwing a posh party.

I sighed. She was a talker, and she worked at home. I couldn't help but feel some sympathy. "Dex decided that I'm a sad and pathetic excuse for a person who needs more friends, and that you need to meet more people, and so he set us up?"

"Sort of. I think I'm the one who's sad and pathetic and needs more friends." She rolled her eyes. "He's familiar with the women who used to be my friends. They're not awesome."

"Which makes me the one needing to meet more

people." Only slightly better, but still kind of offensive.

Her lips quirked, like she was reading my mind and loving that I was ready to give Dex a smackdown. "He told me you just moved here."

"That's true. A few months ago from Houston."

"And that you seemed like you might be a little shy," she added.

No argument there. I made an impulsive decision and closed my laptop. "How does coffee sound?"

Her answering smile was blinding.

"Good, but a boozy brunch sounds better. I know a place with an amazing menu." She gave me a sort of quick up-down look that I'd have missed if I wasn't a natural observer of people. "Ah, assuming you eat carbs?"

I almost laughed, but managed to keep a straight face. "Are you calling me skinny?"

Her eyes got huge and her cheeks pink. "No. Unless you want me to?"

Since her cheeks were getting pinker by the moment, I cut her a break and let out the smile I'd been holding back. "I eat carbs. I have a fast metabolism." I also ran and worked out, but that wasn't any of Taylor's business.

"Ugh, I already hate you and want to be you." She grinned. "The perfect beginning to a friendship."

I laughed. How could I not? She was sweet and she was funny, and she didn't mind throwing Dex under the bus in a not too horrible way. All things which inclined me to like her. And since I currently had exactly one friend in Austin, I decided to go with my gut and give her a chance—even though Dex had sent her my way out of either pity or self-interest, the ass.

When I told her I'd walked, she offered to drive.

Surprise, surprise. The adorably cute, petite woman drove an adorably cute, petite car. It was pastel green and looked like it had just gotten a wax.

The interior was just as pristine.

"I swear there's almost a new car smell in here. I love your car."

She wrinkled her nose. "Thanks. I don't get to drive it much, because Bain doesn't find it very comfortable. I'm actually thinking of selling it."

Sounded like she and this Bain guy were living in each other's pockets if they were driving everywhere together. Also, what an ass, to make her feel like her car wasn't up to snuff. "Let me know if you do. Seriously. I really like it."

With a twitch of her lips, she said, "I can feel your disapproval. Bain's six four."

"Fair enough," I murmured.

What I was really thinking was more along the lines of: what was it about really tall men and really short women? But I didn't know Taylor well enough to voice that particular thought.

Not that I was tall at five six, but still, there seemed to be a dearth of men taller than me in heels. To be fair, I hadn't worn heels in a while, but it was the principle of the thing.

Eh, not really. I just liked tall men.

Dex was definitely taller than me in heels. No contest.

"You're totally thinking about your sexy lumber-jack right now, aren't you?" Taylor's smirk made her a lot less cute. "Ha! I knew it. That look on your face, it's priceless."

"How exactly did you end up coming to the library for a play date?" I couldn't help but use the word. It was so perfect. I definitely felt like a kid being set up with a potential friend.

"Oh, my. That's sort of a long story." She sighed. "One that involves a cheating dick, a skinny bitch who actually turned out to be quite nice, a little body-shaming, and a lot of slut shaming."

I stared. It was kind of a lot.

Then I smiled, because this shit was book gold. "Tell me everything."

Which was how we ended up chatting about all the things over brunch and booze. Taylor just waved a hand when she ordered her second drink. "Bain will sort it all out. I already sent him a text telling him he's responsible for transportation." She leaned close, and I could see her pupils were large and her cheeks quite pink—and that was just from one drink. "I never take the afternoon off. Like ever. Not even for hot dragon sex." She blushed bright red at that little slip, which she needn't have, because what the hell was dragon sex? Then she said, "Since we're here and I'm not about to go crunch numbers... Did I mention I'm a bookkeeper?"

I nodded. She had.

"Well, I can't crunch numbers like this, and we're having a drunk girls' brunch, so I'm getting drunk. Not drunkity drunk, just toasty tipsy."

Oh, my. Taylor was a talker when sober. A little drunk, she was a woman who would spill all the tea. Gotcha, Dex. Before we parted ways, I was getting the scoop on my nerdy-hot library guy.

But first—"Tell me about the cheating dick. And the skinny bitch. But mostly tell me about the shits who body-shamed you, because they were definitely shits. And women. No man is ever saying a bad word about..." I looked her up and down, the implication obvious even to a drunk woman.

It was rude as hell to comment on her physical appearance. Even if I didn't say the words, my meaning was clearly implied. But how could I not? She was a knockout by anyone's standards, and too "toasty tipsy" to take offense.

And who said shit like *toasty tipsy*? Taylor was awesome.

"Aww. I knew I liked you. You're sooo sweet." She scrunched up her nose and made a cutesy face. "Like honeysuckle: hidden, but darling when found."

That analogy didn't exactly track, but she was halfway into her second champagne cocktail, and these were the kind with alcohol, not juice, mixed in. Hence a cocktail and not a mimosa. Girl knew how to party, even if she didn't do it often.

But these sweet assumptions she was making about me, definitely wrong. "I think you're looking through rose-tinted champagne glasses."

She wrinkled her nose again. "You and Bain would totally get along. Oh!" She perked up. "No, you and Dex are definitely gonna get along." Then she winked. Really awkwardly.

It was hilarious.

"Tell me about the dick."

And that was all it took. I got a fiction-worthy story of cheating (that would be the cheating dick of an ex-fiancé) and love (that would the man-mountain known as Bain) and redemption (that would be the skinny bitch who turned out to be cool and clueless that there was a fiancée). That last bit was an unexpected twist, because the redeeming wasn't from an expected character.

"You should totally go out for coffee with the skinny bitch. She sounds like the best kind of bitch. The not bitchy kind."

"Right?" She leaned forward for emphasis, swaying slightly. But did appear on board with my idea. "And maybe I should stop calling her the skinny bitch?"

I laughed, because that was funny as hell, and I'd had two drinks myself. "Yeah, probably a good idea. What's her name?"

"Susie." Another nose wrinkle. "She's like you, all fit and slinky and svelte."

As a writer, I was fairly sure women weren't slinky, but hey—what did I know? Maybe it was slang. Or a drunk Taylor word. Probably that second one.

Also, I was wearing my usual writing gear, the mother of all sweaters. Fluffy and warm and huge, the thing hung past my ass and swallowed me. Not sure how she could tell whether I was slinky.

"You have her number, right?" Taylor had mentioned running into the skinny bitch, aka Susie, after she and Bain started dating.

"Yep." She popped the P, then slid her phone toward me.

I slid it back. "Unlock, please."

And she did. That was how trusting—or toasted —she was. I was definitely ordering her a flavored club soda in a cocktail glass when the waitress came by again.

I found Susie under SUSIE: WILLIAM'S EX. "I'm texting her. 'Kay?"

She nodded. "Meant to. Keep forgetting."

She blushed, and I couldn't help wondering if dragon sex was on her brain. Google and I would be speaking later, and if the internet couldn't get me sorted, I had another source or two to ask. Online writer friends were great for research. Also, I was writing a book with a were-dragon. I should know what the hell dragon sex was.

After identifying myself as Taylor's brunch buddy, I tapped my way to a Sunday coffee appointment at ten. I figured Taylor might be rough tomorrow, depending on how the rest of her day went today, but the following day she should be okay. I hoped. Otherwise I was going to feel bad. A little like I fed a kid too much candy on Halloween, except there was alcohol involved and we were still a few weeks shy of that particular holiday. The kid part was spot on, though. Probably the spark of joyful innocence I saw in her. The sad thing was that there wasn't anything inherently juvenile in that; I'd just lost mine when I was a child.

Her phone vibrated in my hand, chasing away maudlin thoughts.

"Susie's thrilled and asked if I'm coming."

"Absolutely." Taylor sipped on her third drink.

Dammit. I'd missed the waitress while I was fiddling with her phone. She was slippery for a drunk person.

"All right. You're all set up to meet your cheating dick-face ex's ex-hookup." I raised my eyebrows. "Your life is a little weird."

Which warmed my heart. I loved it when I discovered other people didn't have completely normal, white-bread-with-American-cheese-and-no-crust lives.

After growing up with my dad, I'd have thought

everyone was into doughy, undercooked, tasteless, processed food...metaphorically.

"Oh yeah." She nodded like that was no big deal. And the warmth in my chest expanded.

"You're a really fun drunk." When she frowned, I amended to, "toasty tipsy."

"Ah, I might be at fucks drunk." She squinted at her drink. "I've never had more than one of these before."

I wasn't sure I wanted to know what fucks drunk was.

"Fuck, yeah. I'm drunk." She made gimme hands and reached for her phone.

I covered it just long enough to ask, "Is this that moment when I try to prevent you from sending inappropriate texts while inebriated?"

"Hell, no." She smiled as she looked up at me from under her lashes. "I'm just gonna warn Bain."

I laughed out loud as I handed her the phone. I hadn't had this much fun in ages.

Which was sad. Not that Taylor wasn't a blast, just sad that the most fun I'd had since moving here was with a woman I'd met less than two hours ago.

When she was done texting and blushing, I said, "Tell me about Dex."

"Oh, awesome! We're doing this!" She looked

around, made a face, then said in a much quieter voice, "What do you want to know? There's the obvious: the nice laugh, the nice beard, the nice eyes, the nice—" She waved her hand. "—everything else."

I wouldn't have gone with nice, but then, I also wasn't in a relationship with another man. "I was thinking more about the parts I can't see."

Her eyes widened, then she wrinkled her nose. "Oh, you mean like his personality."

Ha! This lady. But I just asked in a practical tone, "Unless you want to tell me about his other less visible parts?"

"No!" Her eyes narrowed, squinting suspiciously. "You're totally messing with me."

"I am absolutely messing with you."

"Whew. Because I really can't talk about Dex's junk. Pretty sure Bain would pick up on it psychically and get his man feelings hurt." She smiled sweetly. "But I can talk about what a nice guy Dex is."

"Nice, huh?"

She slurped the last of her drink. This time I wasn't going to miss the waitress. She seemed to catch on, because she grinned. "Don't worry. That was my last one. But yes, Dex is nice. You wanna go out with a guy who isn't? I did that. It sucks."

"Yeah, no arguments. That guy sucked." I ran my finger along the sweating exterior of my half-full glass. Unlike Taylor, I hadn't chugged my second round. "So when you say nice, you mean not the kind of guy who cheats."

"Definitely not. Dex wouldn't. No way." She looked seriously wigged out by the idea.

"You know him that well, huh?" I couldn't help it; she was just so bothered by even the idea, and so emphatic in her denial, and yet, friendship and romantic relationships were worlds apart. Dex could be a loyal friend and yet a complete sleaze when it came to women.

"Look, I'm sure he gets around. He's hot. But I can tell you with absolute certainty that if Dex is in a relationship, he's going to be faithful. It's how they're built."

"They?"

"Bain, Dex, Archer." When I shook my head, she said, "I keep forgetting we haven't known each other forever, because it feels like we have. Archer's the other one."

"Ah, right. The other one."

She rolled her eyes. "You know what I mean. They're all really good friends. From way back. Way, *way* back."

So, college buddies. Probably in a frat together. Possibly also an athletic team of some kind. If they were local Texas boys, it would be football, no doubt.

"You think I should go out with him." Not really a question. It seemed pretty obvious that Taylor was pro-Dex. She was dating the guy's college bestie.

"I think that you should do exactly as you like." She leaned forward, suddenly quite serious. "I'm not here to convince you to go out with Dex. I'm here to meet you. I had a feeling we'd get along." Then she rolled her eyes and sighed. "I'm a little psychic. Sounds kooky, but it is what it is, so I try not to ignore the universe when she winks at me."

The fact that I only flinched slightly at the mention of psychic abilities was a sign of how much I liked Taylor. "Not so kooky. My neighbor cast a love spell and told me it found the other half of me."

"No—really?" She rubbed her hands together. "Tell me more. Is he tall, dark, and handsome? Dex is almost as tall as Bain, sort of dark, and definitely handsome...if you're into lumberjacks. Are you into lumberjacks?"

Ignoring the question, I said, "Ah, yeah, she wasn't talking about Dex."

If only. Then maybe I'd avoid another setup with

a nearing fifty, determinedly single bachelor with a strong dislike of romance novels.

"How do you know? Did you meet this mystery man?"

"That's a hard no. She's fixated on one of our neighbors."

"Oh, awkward."

I tapped the table. "See, Mathilde doesn't get it. The potential corner store run-ins, the coffee shop mishaps, there are so many ways that can go wrong. And I don't trust her judgment. She keeps trying to set me up with these completely inappropriate guys."

But instead of commiserating with me, Taylor closed her eyes. She tilted her head, and then wrinkled her nose. When she finally checked back in, she looked a shade more sober than before. "Mathilde Madsen?"

That was weird. How the hell did Taylor know Mathilde?

"Fuck." She made a circle with her finger in the general direction of my face. "That look says yes, which is...fuck."

Since Taylor seemed like the kind of person to most profusely cuss when drunk or in great distress, I was hoping for drunk. Obviously she was inebri-

ated, but I was hopeful she wasn't also freaked out...
even though she looked it.

Damn. She was looking more sober by the
minute.

"You know Mathilde?" I mean, obviously she
knew Mathilde. I just wanted to know how, and also
why she was looking so wiggy about it.

"I know of her. She's Dex's neighbor."

It took maybe two seconds for me to make the
appropriate connections. "Okay, so Dex lives in my
neighborhood. Not shocking, since we both go to the
same branch library. And maybe Dex is the guy she's
been trying to hook me up with. Maybe."

But she wasn't listening. She was texting. Who
was she texting? *What* was she texting?

"Whoa. Stop with the phone already."

She looked up curiously. "I'm not messaging
Dex. Just Bain."

"Who is Dex's buddy."

She frowned harder. "Yes, but seriously, this is
a... I don't know what it is. That's why I'm texting
Bain."

She got a reply that surprised her. She looked up
at me, and I'd swear I saw a hint of concern on her
face.

She quickly looked down and tapped away on

her phone. Then she wrinkled her nose and said, "But I've had three drinks."

She wasn't talking to me. She was talking to the phone.

"You okay over there?"

"No. No, I am not okay." She inhaled deeply, met my gaze with an intent, serious look on her face, then cringed and lifted her hand. "I lied. I do need another drink."

"But do you really?"

"Girl, you have no idea. I'll just order us a pitcher and the boys can pour us into the car later."

I was starting to wonder if maybe Taylor had a bit of a drinking problem. Maybe more than a bit.

And what she said next sealed the deal. "Mathilde's a retired love witch, and Bain thinks you might be Dex's mate. Uh, like a fated soul mate." Then she waved her hand at our server. "I need a pitcher of Pomegranate Royale. Please. Pretty please?"

Witches and fated soul mates.

There was a little psychic, and there was...*that*.

Nope.

I'd get up and walk out the door—rideshare was a stranded gal's friend—but no way could I leave Taylor here alone in the state she was in. Just because she was a complete lunatic didn't mean I liked her any less than five minutes ago or that I wanted anything bad to happen to her.

So I sighed, declined a refill, and nodded as drunkity drunk Taylor told me again that she was psychic, and she just had a feeling about me. (Feelings which seemed to escalate the more she drank.)

And that she just had a feeling about me and Dex ending up in the same neighborhood. (Spoiler: it was called a tight real estate market and a limited number of small craftsmen-style homes.)

And she just had a feeling about me and Dex as a couple. (Spoiler: that definitely wasn't happening, because Dex and his friends believed in the fantasy of magic, and I wanted no part of that. Not after my childhood. Not with my imagination and the wild places it could take me if I wasn't careful.)

And that she was just so glad to meet me, because she really needed a girlfriend who didn't belong to the mean girls club. (Spoiler: that about broke my heart, because so did I, but she and I couldn't be that for each other.)

9

DEX

I got a text to meet Bain at Taylor's favorite brunch spot.

That couldn't be good.

That meant that Taylor and Kaylee had gotten plastered and needed a ride home. Or worse, because Bain could have handled the transportation of two drunk women without me.

Taylor must have scared Kaylee with tales of magic and dragons.

Shit.

When I'd set up the whole Taylor bumping into Kaylee scenario, I hadn't envisioned *that*. I'd trusted Taylor to have more sense. Then again, I also hadn't pictured a tipsy Taylor hanging out with Kaylee.

Bain's woman could not hold her alcohol.

Couldn't she have a nice chat? Make a friend. Maybe slip in a nice word or two about me—or not —but at least stay sober for her first meeting with Kaylee. How hard was that?

Chelsea's cold nose nudged my hand. She could tell I was tense.

She wasn't wrong. Calm eluded me at the moment. I ran my hand through her tawny fur. "All right. You can come. Let's go."

The magic words. She was through the door to the garage and standing at the back of the Tahoe, tail wagging happily, before I could rethink my choice.

Ten minutes later, I arrived to find Bain in the parking lot, leaning against the side of his vehicle, obviously waiting for me.

"What?" he said when I rolled the driver's window down. Then with a dour look my way, he added, "I'm not going in there alone."

"What happened?" I fiddled with the windows so there was enough air for Chelsea, told her I'd be right back when Bain didn't immediately reply, and then got out to deal with whatever mess his mate had made.

Once the Tahoe door was shut, he said, "You know that Kaylee is friends with Mathilde?"

Now it was my turn to lean against my car. "No. I

didn't know that." Although it might explain why the two women owned matching sweaters.

What was Kaylee doing befriending my seemingly eighty-some-odd-year-old neighbor? And how the hell had they even met?

"Yeah. They're neighbors." He gave me a significant look, because if Mathilde and Kaylee were neighbors, then Kaylee and I were neighbors. "She cast a love spell for your girl."

Now that was surprising. "Mathilde is retired."

"*Long* retired."

A distinctly unpleasant thought planted itself in my head: that the spell had worked.

My chest tightened, and I felt the rush of blood in my ears like I did before I fucked someone up.

Except I wasn't a soldier anymore and I didn't resort to violence to solve my problems. I was calm. I was no Berserker.

Chelsea's whine clued me in that I wasn't calm. Not even close. I went to the rear passenger window and spoke soothingly to Chels. When she was quiet, I turned back to Bain, steeling myself for bad news, and trying to convince myself I wasn't about to end some random guy's life. "Who did the spell land on?"

"You, you dumbass. Who else?"

The relief I felt was out of proportion to the situation. I barely knew Kaylee. Also, what the hell did I care what a love spell predicted when the witch casting it was Mathilde? Nothing magical that woman did could be trusted. It had been so long since she'd worked magic that I forgot she was a witch.

"Yeah, right." I refrained from rolling my eyes, but only just. "Mathilde hasn't practiced for over a century, and we both know why."

Her magic had gone all wrong, and in a particularly spectacular way.

"Doesn't mean this spell didn't work."

"That's exactly what the fuck it means," I snapped. There was a growly edge to my voice that I didn't like. I almost sounded like Bain. Pre-Taylor Bain.

Shit. Not a good look on me. And not the "me" I was going for this century.

"Lost some of your zen there, buddy?"

He was right. My calm had abandoned me. Because this was fucked.

I was angry that Fate would tease me in such a way. Frustrated that I wasn't likely to find what Bain had. Pissed that I was broken and didn't know why or how to fix it.

Not calm. Sure as hell not zen.

Chelsea whined again from the back of the Tahoe.

I breathed in deeply through my nose and pushed out my breath through pursed lips, slowing my exhalation.

A few rounds and I could speak without sounding like a pissed-off Neanderthal. "It's okay, Chels." I opened the back door so I could scratch under her chin, which was therapeutic in its own way. Once she was reassured that I wasn't about to lose my shit—not something she had much experience with, hence the whining—I closed the door.

"You good?" Bain asked, sounding more amused than concerned.

He could go fuck himself. He had a mate. He could shift.

I flipped him the finger in response. But I did it casually. I could be calm and crass at the same time, no problem.

"Besides the fact that Kaylee and Mathilde are bosom buddies, what else is going on?"

"Taylor told your girl she was psychic and that Mathilde was a love witch, so maybe she should listen to Mathilde's predictions."

I groaned. There wasn't a lot of tolerance for

magic these days and even less belief in it. "Now she'll never go out with me."

"I don't know. Some women seem to like you for some odd reason, so you never know."

"Asshole."

He grinned. "Just wanted you to know that magic's already in the equation."

"But not dragons."

"No. You ready?" But he didn't wait for a response.

I stared at his back, then followed. Maybe it wouldn't be so bad. She could be open-minded, maybe even dabbled in crystals or tarot. They were both making a mainstream comeback.

I walked inside directly behind Bain and caught his sharp inhale, indicative of surprise. A second later, he muttered, "I guess you know your girl has magic."

As if I'd miss that. I dismissed the fact that I hadn't noticed, not until I'd shaken hands with her. But that was then. Now? Holy hell, that wasn't at all what I'd detected. The bit of magic I felt inside her, what I saw now was easily ten times more powerful.

There was no overlooking her spark now.

There was also no missing her expression. I'd seen it before on others. Closed, skeptical, distant.

She'd already decided: she was on one side of the fence, and we were on the other.

It didn't really matter what created that line between us. We were delusional, religious fanatics, gullible—again, it didn't matter. The takeaway was that the fence was firmly in place, and she'd put herself on the opposite side.

Taylor took one look at the expression on my face and pointed at her mate. "He made me do it."

Wild guess, Taylor was talking about spilling her magical guts.

Bain didn't normally insert himself into private matters. Then his ex died, and I'd shown up in Austin with Archer demanding he get his shit together. Maybe this was payback.

Which was bullshit. He'd been desperately in need of an intervention. He'd been wasted and flying around burning shit, and then he'd been drugged by a Van Helsing. The same Van Helsing who'd texted a picture of his comatose, vulnerable ass passed out on a bed in his cabin.

He'd deserved more than an intervention. He should be glad that was all Archer and I did.

I, however, did not deserve an intervention or his meddling. I hadn't destroyed property or passed out for several days after being darted by a Van Helsing.

"Kaylee." She wouldn't quite meet my eyes. *Son of a bitch.* "Can I offer you a lift home?"

"No, I've got it covered. I ordered a rideshare when I saw you in the parking lot." She looked past my shoulder. "There it is now."

She turned to Taylor and hugged her, whispering, "Take care," into her ear before walking out the door.

"Oh, Dex, I'm sorry. I had no idea she'd react that way." Taylor looked wrecked. "It was different for me. I just sort of didn't believe and then did. Kaylee shut down, like she couldn't go there. Not even a little bit." She lowered her voice to a theatrical whisper-shout. "And I didn't even mention the part about dragons."

Ironically, *I'd* been Taylor's introduction to dragons. She'd spotted me in dragon form on her front lawn when I was cloaked. And now I couldn't call forth my dragon to save my life.

Fuck you, Fate.

There was a mostly full pitcher of some alcoholic beverage on the table.

Looking around, no one seemed overly concerned by our antics. Just a typical Friday in central Austin. "Let's finish that pitcher of..."

"Pomegranate Royale," Taylor replied with a hopeful look. "I really could use another drink."

Bain looked overtly skeptical but didn't say a word.

I might not be getting laid in the foreseeable future, but at least I could make sure Bain wasn't either. Sometimes it was the small—even petty—pleasures in life that got one through the day. After I sat down, I reached for the pitcher. "Let me pour you a glass, Taylor."

Bain scowled, but again, didn't say a word.

I smiled back, but there wasn't any joy in it.

I liked Kaylee. I didn't really know her, but I'd wanted to. Something about her, she was—

"Don't give up so easily, you sorry bastard." Bain settled into one of the too-small chairs. He looked up and a waitress magically appeared. We had that effect on waitstaff. Could be our size, but I suspected they could sniff out a good tipper from twenty yards. "Can we have a menu?"

When she was gone, I said, "Haven't you ever heard the term no means no?"

Taylor stopped sipping long enough to say, "Hey, don't quote me out of context." Then she frowned. "I'm not sure she did say no."

"She didn't. Also, it's pretty obvious she has no

idea she's a witch." Bain looked over his shoulder, hunting for the server and the accompanying promised menu.

"Nooo. Really? No way." Taylor pointed an accusing finger at me. Her southern manners never seemed to dissuade that rude finger of hers. "You didn't tell me that."

"Because she wasn't. Maybe isn't."

Bain raised his eyebrows, then accepted a menu from the waitress who appeared at his shoulder. He immediately opened it to the carb-filled section of waffles and pancakes. "Hey, honey, what do you think about some pancakes?"

Taylor snatched the menu from his hands, and he surreptitiously inched her cocktail out of reach.

Damn, he was good.

While Taylor was occupied picking out her carb choice, I explained that Kaylee hadn't been in possession of that much magic when I'd originally met her.

"Right." Bain's tone implied the opposite.

"Seriously. I could tell she had a little magic when I shook her hand, otherwise zip." I could see his skepticism and knew immediately where he was going next. "No, my sight isn't broken."

"Huh. That's odd."

"Yes, it is."

"You should talk to Mathilde." Taylor's voice emerged from behind the menu. She was still dithering over which particular carb would suit her.

I'd planned to, if only to have a chat about her poor life choices of late, but I was interested to know drunk Taylor's reasoning. "Why?"

"To find out if she *really* cast a love spell. It sounded like maybe she'd set Kaylee up with some other guys, so maybe she was just *telling* her she cast a love spell, thinking that would persuade her to give you a try." She lowered the menu. "She'd have to have lady balls of titanium to fiddle with real love magic again after what happened."

I hadn't a clue if Mathilde had lady balls, titanium or otherwise, because I'd sort of forgotten she was anything other than what she appeared to be: an eighty-plus-year-old neighbor who waved whenever I jogged by her house.

She was a technically still a witch, even if she shouldn't be after—"Oh, shit."

"Yeah, I was just thinking the same thing." Bain looked completely unamused for the first time today.

"What'd I miss?" Taylor whisper-shouted in

Bain's ear. She had a poor grasp of volume when drunk.

"Mathilde is a love witch, which makes her a witch, which makes her capable of—"

"Ohmigawd! She hexed you!"

10

DEX

Austin folks tended to be accustomed to the occasional oddity. Drunken shouts of witchcraft blended into the background, especially in a place known for its boozy brunch.

I was pretty sure Bain would leave a ridiculously large tip to make up for our shenanigans.

Not that I knew for sure, because I'd left before the bill arrived.

Mathilde and I needed to have a chat.

Since I had Chelsea in the car with me, I went home first.

For the entirety of the ten-minute drive, she shot accusatory looks my way. Either because we were headed home without a stop off at a park or because I was an edgy ball of tension.

"Sorry, Chels. No P-A-R-K today."

She yipped in response.

Yeah, my dog could spell. Mostly the important shit like park, walk, run, ball. She also knew the names of her toys. She was basically brilliant.

Because I'd both deprived her of a treat and mentioned the P-A-R-K word without delivering, I stopped long enough to throw the ball for her about a hundred times before I headed over to Mathilde's house.

She was next door but for two houses. In other words, too damn close to be fomenting chaos without my knowledge.

I should have known she was up to something. She'd taken to gardening on my running days. I run every other day, so it's not a regular schedule. The woman was keeping an eye on me.

"But she's retired," I muttered as I headed to the door.

Chelsea, following on my heels, huffed out a canine sigh.

I held out my hand. "Wait. I'll be back after I deal with a deranged love witch whose magic has been known to fritz epically."

Chelsea's eyebrows lifted and she tilted her head, giving her an eagerly worried appearance.

"Right. TMI." I scratched behind her ear, then left.

Were love witches psychic? Mathilde was waiting for me. Or someone. Her curtains twitched as I approached her door, and it opened before I knocked.

"Dexter. What a lovely surprise."

"Dex," I replied. "And is it really?"

"Dex. Yes, I suppose that's more modern, and there's also that TV serial killer that shares your name. Too close to home, I suppose."

I eyed her askance. I wasn't anything like a *serial killer*. I'd been a soldier. Not at all the same thing, even to scatty retired love witches with fritzing magic.

"Don't look so offended. It's a very popular show."

And now she was just messing with me. "May I come in, please?"

She smiled benevolently and stepped to the side with a sweeping gesture. "Of course. Welcome to my home."

She indicated the kitchen, which was visible because her house was much smaller than mine and open concept. The entry flowed to the living room which flowed to a dining area which flowed into the kitchen. I liked it. Small, cramped houses made me feel like I was in a cage.

She made a disapproving sound from behind me. "You're not looking like yourself, Dex."

After she got done checking out my ass, she must have noticed the hex that was interfering with my magic.

Her hex, I was willing to bet a hefty sum. Couldn't the woman even recognize her own work?

She indicated I take a seat at the bar. "I'll just make us a pot of tea." Seeing my scowl, she said, "Just tea."

"Since you're not supposed to be doing magic, that might be wise."

And now it was her turn to frown. "I don't know what you've heard, but my retirement was voluntary. I was neither stripped nor bound."

A shame.

I didn't hide my thoughts well, because she said, "Keep that attitude up and I will put something in your tea."

"Like you haven't done enough."

She flicked the switch on her electric kettle. "You can thank me later."

"Thank you?" I lowered my voice, to make absolutely certain I wasn't yelling, but the grim note was there. "I'm broken."

"Bound," she corrected. "I can see how your sort would see it that way, as a deficit rather than a temporary hurdle. But that's nothing to do...with me."

That pause was telling. It was like she was just realizing that whatever magic she'd wrought—and I was guessing she'd gone well beyond a locating love spell—had resulted in unintended consequences.

I'd been like this for *weeks*.

She'd seen me jogging at least half a dozen times, probably more.

The tea kettle clicked off, and she didn't move. She bit her lip.

Finally, she said, "Oops?"

I growled.

Better than a roar, but it still didn't go over well.

"You can just stop with the angry dragon noises right now. I didn't do it on purpose, and my heart was in the right place."

Thoughtlessly or with intent, did it matter? The result was the same. She'd hexed me. I couldn't shift. No doubt Mathilde was responsible. It took strong magic to bind a dragon, and as erratic as hers might be, Mathilde had magic aplenty. She was the offspring of a demon and a god, two magical beings. Most witches resulted from demon–human pairings, which often diluted power in the offspring.

She scowled back at me. "Milk with your tea?"

"Yes." I swallowed a sigh, but didn't lighten the intense look of displeasure I was sporting when I added, "Please."

We drank our tea in silence, me perched on a barstool and her leaning against the kitchen counter on the other side of the bar.

We'd made it silently through half a good-sized mug when she finally said, "I'm sorry—but I think I know how it happened."

"You practiced magic when you should have stayed retired?"

Her lips thinned and she kept her silence. Dammit. I should have bit my tongue. But I was rightfully pissed. Hell, I was righteously pissed. She'd *broken* me. My dragon was my other half. An integral part of me was trapped inside my body, unable to be set free.

It was only the last few days that I'd truly begun to feel the strain. I thought it would have taken longer. I'd once gone a few months without shifting and hadn't experienced any ill effects.

But then it had been my choice.

It was being broken, less than whole, that was eating at me.

"Will you attempt to be civil?"

I shouldn't have to. *I* hadn't accidentally hexed a dragon.

Her eyes narrowed, but then she sighed. "I'd forgotten how prideful your sort are. I'll take your silence for assent."

I waited patiently for an explanation. I could be patient. Blue sky, the air's embrace as it lifted and held me. Basking in the sun's rays, soaking up the heat as I sprawled uncloaked on a huge rock. I could be patient if I crutched off some of my meditation imagery.

"Are you feeling better now?" Mathilde asked with a smirk she shouldn't feel confident enough to display.

No one feared us anymore. It was a real problem. Bain had a run-in with the local rat shifters because they hadn't respected us, and now this.

"I didn't know it would be you." At the look on my face, she rolled her eyes. "You dragons. You think the sun rises and sets on your colorful scales. Just like peacocks, pretty but no brains. I cast a love spell for *Kaylee*. You just happened to be on the receiving end."

"If you didn't target me, then how did you end up binding me?"

"I didn't. The spell did. I gave it a little kick." She looked down at her half-full teacup. And it was to that milky-brown substance that she directed her next comment. "I wanted to be sure it worked, so I dusted off an old book of spells and, well, there you go."

She'd boosted a locating love spell with...something. "What did you combine with the love spell?"

She looked at me sharply. "Does it matter?"

Blue skies, the air's embrace... "Yes, Mathilde. It does matter, because I'd like for you to unbind my dragon."

"No can do."

The rumble started low in my gut and crawled its way up to my chest, throat, mouth.

"Don't you dare spit fire in my kitchen."

I swallowed back the nasty sound that wanted to claw its way out. *Think of the rock. The big rock and the sun.* "Dragons don't spit fire. We throw it."

I didn't add that we happened to do that with our tails. Not currently an option for me. A dragon could throw fire in human form...but not when his dragon was bound. I had no fire. Not to spit or throw or make in any way. Because this incompetent witch had broken me.

She waved her hand, as if my lack of fire were some small thing. "Either way, mind your manners in my house. I still have a magical trick or two up my sleeve that works just fine." Her eyes softened. "I truly can't undo it. It was intertwined with the love spell. I thought I was just making sure that the one the spell found was Kaylee's One True Love, but I think it just made her One True Love a little more..." She sighed. "Hell, I'm just going to say it. It made you more palatable to a woman like Kaylee."

This was the first real information she'd shared, however cryptic. I set aside her implication that I was Kaylee's One True Love. The non-dragon version of a mate. A soul mate. That was...impossible. Cruel to tease. Most importantly, not the pressing issue.

"How could binding my dragon possibly change how she sees me? It's not like I fly around Austin flaunting my 'colorful scales.' I walk. I drive. I get around like the other million or so men who live here."

Mathilde gave me a hard look. "What the hell have you been doing the last week? I did everything to give you a chance—and what do you do with it?"

Yeah, everything. Like crippling me. Breaking apart the very underpinnings of who I am. Excellent choice there, Mathilde. Oh, yeah, right. It wasn't a choice. It was an accident.

I was proud of myself for keeping my trap shut. Instead, I very calmly and rationally said, "I have no idea what you're talking about."

She tapped the table with her index finger. "And that's my point. If you'd talked to the girl, gotten to know her, then you wouldn't be so confused."

I scrambled to find some connection, some tie between my dragon and Kaylee's potential interest in me. Between my magic and... her magic? "Is this something to do with the magic she's been hiding away?"

"Not my story to tell." That was a yes.

She took a sip of tea.

I waited.

"You really should talk to her."

"I would, if she were talking to me right now."

She closed her eyes on a deep inhale, then exhaled as if expelling the weight of the world—or one hefty, human-form dragon. "Try harder, you idiot. She's a wonderful person, and she deserves her One True Love—even if it's you."

I grasped the now empty mug and rolled it

between my hands, because blue skies and sun-warmed rocks weren't doing it for me. I felt the need to defend myself. "Have you ever heard of no means no?"

First Taylor, now Mathilde. Weren't they supposed to have Kaylee's back? The sisterhood of women...or something like that.

She eyed me like I'd lost my mind. "This isn't an issue of consent. This is an issue of you fumbling an excellent chance to find your mate. I thought all you dragons longed for your mates."

"She's not my mate." It was a whisper, yet felt like I'd shouted my rejection from the rooftops.

I wasn't *rejecting* her. I just couldn't believe she was the one. Couldn't believe that I was worthy of one. Especially now. I was *broken*, dammit.

"I find you your mate, and this is the thanks I get?"

A good point—if Kaylee was my soul mate.

But she wasn't.

I'd know if she were. There'd be signs. A zing. A spark.

There'd be *something* out of the ordinary.

I rubbed the itch at the back of my neck. Something beyond an insistent desire to get to know her. To learn about her life.

I'd sent my best friend's mate to meet her. And if I was honest with myself, not to chat up my virtues. Taylor wasn't my biggest fan, given that whole purse violating issue. I was winning her over, but it was an ongoing process.

No, if I was honest, I'd done it because I thought they'd hit it off. Kaylee seemed lonely. Taylor was a really nice woman who needed more friends.

Since when did I make such massive leaps in logic? I just met Kaylee. She'd lightly stalked me at the library, and I'd ogled her in return. I didn't really know her. I could guess that she was shy based on her behavior toward me, but I didn't know that she was lonely.

Except, I was sure she was.

Just like I was sure she and Taylor would hit it off. And they had, as evidenced by their brunch date. Even if it hadn't ended well, Kaylee had agreed to it. More chance than she'd given me...

"Wrapped your tiny peacock brain around it yet?"

I set the mug aside. "I'm not agreeing."

This time it was her silence that prompted me to speak.

I swallowed a sigh. "I'm not disagreeing."

"Yeah. That's what I thought."

I might have met my mate, an event I'd spent much of my life both hoping for and despairing would ever happen, and here I was a wingless, fire-less, practically powerless mess.

My jaw was clenching, my fist balled. Blue skies and warm rocks definitely weren't cutting it—because I was fucking broken when I could least afford to be. "You have to fix me."

Pity softened her gaze. "I can't. I didn't bind you. It's a side effect of the spell I cast."

"So reverse *that* spell. The one you cast that made the side effect."

"I can't. It's already run its course. There's nothing to reverse."

Fuck. I knew she was right. The spell that made me this way no longer existed. But that didn't mean there wasn't a fix. A loophole. A way to undo the side effects.

With magic, there was always balance. What could be done, could be undone.

"You have to know how to fix it."

She pursed her lips. "I don't know. Give me some time, and I'll think on it."

It wasn't like I could pressure her. The witch was as old as I was. And at the moment, even with her glitchy, unpredictable magic, more powerful.

I brought to bear the only leverage I still had. "You don't want to make an enemy of the dragons."

She didn't blink. Didn't look worried. She did look a little sad. "No, I don't. More than that, I want Kaylee happy. That poor girl deserves her happily ever after, and I will skewer your tiny peacock brain if you fuck this up."

I'd written myself into a corner.

It was like on some level I'd guessed that Dex was one of *those* people. The ones who believed in psychics and love spells. Because I'd written him—or rather Drake, his fictional alter ego —into a book filled with magic. It was a corner, because I didn't want to write about dragons with blue-green scales.

But it was that or not write at all.

Writers talked about characters hijacking their stories, and I always thought I understood that concept. But I hadn't a clue. Not till now.

Dex, in the form of were-dragon Drake, had stolen my story and was making off with it as I typed.

It was so frustrating.

Clearly, this book wouldn't be the next in my series of loosely connected, romantic suspense novels. Dammit. I was supposed to be working on a cop-saves-lady-who-saves-him story, not a dragon-saves-lady-who-saves-him story.

But I'd woken up this morning, skipped the library for my writing shed in the backyard, and proceeded to stare at the walls.

Just to test a theory, I closed out the romantic suspense project and opened the dreaded Drake story—and immediately added two thousand words before I realized it was time for lunch.

What that test revealed was pretty simple. I wasn't in a corner. I didn't have writer's block. I could opt to work on my romantic suspense and stare at the walls or I could finish the damn were-dragon project.

While thinking about Dex.

While *fantasizing* about Dex.

And also immersed in a world where magic was a real, everyday occurrence.

I was feeling pretty violent despite the fact that I'd gotten a good chunk of my projected word count done for the day, because...

I didn't want to write about Dex. Or dragons. Or magic.

When I'd started the book, I didn't think it was a big deal. I ignored my dad's voice in the back of my head saying it wasn't smart, because it was *just a fiction story*. No problem.

But suddenly real people in my life were spouting off about love spells and psychic impressions. My only friend in Austin was apparently some kind of witch, and not the sort that embraced a particular spiritual philosophy. The kind who cast love spells. And when she'd told me that, I hadn't even thought much of it. Just that she was a little kooky.

Same with Taylor. Just a little bit off the wall.

I hadn't been comfortable with their beliefs, but I hadn't had any sort of negative reaction like with Dex. I'd been slowly sucked in, one step at a time, and this damn book was just the freaking icing.

I let out a frustrated scream.

Fully finished writing sheds with good windows and decent insolation were great for that.

When I'd finished yelling, I realized it hadn't helped at all. I was just as frustrated and angry as before.

Usually when I got this way about a story... Actually, who was I kidding? I never got *this* emotional about a story. Not heart-thudding, panicked-tightening-in-my-chest angry. But when I'd gotten frustrated in the past, I'd simply reached out to one of my many virtual writer friends and we'd talked through it.

I wasn't about to do that. I could just picture it: so I met this guy and he's into magic, but that's a taboo topic for me, so I can't go there even though he's insanely hot and the singular inspiration for all of my writing right now.

I knew what my two closest friends would say. If he wasn't a realistic long-term option, fuck him out of my system, use him as inspiration for the book, and start a new pen name that writes all the dragon books. Problem solved.

My two closest friends also happened to know that while my writing was my full-time profession and supported me, I actually had a trust fund that I could fall back on. I'd never relied on it. Never even touched the money, but it was there if I needed it, and that gave me flexibility to basically write all the dragon books I wanted even if they weren't on my writing schedule or in my marketing plan.

But that money was a whole different can of worms. Not inconsiderable funds left to me by the mother who'd abandoned me as an infant. *I'm not really into babies. Here's some cash for the kid and here's some for you. Hope it makes you feel better about raising a child alone.*

Not that she'd said as much to my dad. I didn't think. I didn't actually know, because my father never spoke of her. Not what color her hair was, though I suspected dark like mine since Dad was blond. Not where they'd met or how long they'd known each other, though obviously long enough for him to knock her up and her to have me.

It was a touchy subject for him. I didn't even know about the money until I turned twenty-five and Dad had basically handed it over. All he'd said was, "Your mother set up this trust for you. I added what she gave me for your care. It's all yours now."

That conversation made it clear Dad's feelings toward the woman who'd birthed and abandoned me. He hadn't spent her child support payments, even when I was young and I knew finances were tight.

He really, really didn't like to talk about her.

Hell, she could be dead for all I knew.

I let out another scream.

Then I calmly closed my laptop—after saving my work, because I wasn't a monster. Even unplanned were-dragon stories deserved that much.

And then I called my father.

"Kaylee." He answered the phone with a worried tone.

My dad did that a lot. Worry, about me.

I took a breath, then dove in headfirst before I could chicken out. "Tell me about my mother."

A heavy pause followed. I'd love to see his face.

"Why are you asking about her now?" Again, worry oozed in every word.

A more relevant question would be why I never demanded he tell me everything. Why I didn't beg for every scrap of information about her. And failing that, why I didn't at least get her damn name.

I didn't even know my mother's name.

She was this faceless person who'd cared just enough to give birth to me, then walked away.

"Just answer the question, Dad."

"I don't think this is a conversation we should have over the phone."

That response I'd expected. "Fine. I'll drive to Houston. I can leave in twenty minutes."

He sighed. It was a sad, defeated sound. But when he replied, I realized I'd misunderstood. "You'd tell me if you were having any...issues, wouldn't you?"

He wasn't caving. He was just convinced I was two steps away from insanity. That I was back to the behaviors of my childhood, allowing my imagination to take me so far from reality that I created dust bunny pets with purple eyes and thought our neighbor's daughter-in-law had fairy wings.

I'd actually forgotten all about Mrs. Neal's daughter-in-law's wings.

"I'm not having the kind of issues you're talking about, Dad. I'm only seeing exactly what's in front of me. No more, no less."

"That's good. Good to hear. Keep your feet planted in reality. That's my girl."

And all of a sudden that anger I'd felt about my runaway story was directed straight at my dad. He'd stolen a part of my childhood. He took away the magic, because he was scared.

Sure, my imagination had been more vivid than most children's, but had there ever truly been any harm in it?

"You know what, Dad? I don't think you're the person I should be talking to right now. I..." I swallowed whatever else had been on the tip of my tongue. Words couldn't be unsaid. And whatever else I'd learned in my life, I knew to my very core that words held power. So I spoke the one truth I knew wouldn't harm the dearest person in my life. "I love you, Dad. We'll talk soon."

A fraught, brief silence followed, broken finally when he replied, "I love you, too, Kaylee-girl. So much."

Yeah, I knew he did. If only he trusted me in equal measure.

I stared at my phone, an idea bubbling up. One that was long overdue.

I opened my laptop and turned to my reliable friend Google. Sadly, Google couldn't tell me which private investigator of the many my search retrieved was the best or the most appropriate for the task I had in mind.

I hesitated for a heartbeat, but then I caved. Just because I was put off by Mathilde's life choices didn't change the fact that she was my only real friend in Austin. She'd only ever been good to me. Even her misguided attempts at matchmaking were grounded in her desire to see me happy. And she'd been in the area long enough to just maybe have an idea who could help me.

I picked up my phone and sent her a text: *Any good recommendations for a private investigator?*

Her reply came about as fast as it would take her to type a response. She must have had her phone handy. Not only did she give me a name—Maddie—

she provided a number and offered to make a personal introduction.

After I'd replied that it wasn't necessary and thanked her, she told me to be sure and mention that she'd been the one to pass along Maddie's name.

Since it never hurt to have a personal in, I did exactly that.

The woman who answered the phone—not Maddie, but Leila, Maddie's scheduling assistant— hadn't been especially professional, and she'd made a surprised sound when I mentioned Mathilde Madsen had referred me. But she also hadn't hesitated to set up an appointment with Maddie Van Helsing to discuss the job. Today.

The name set off alarm bells—probably why Mathilde had only given me a first name—but I agreed. I needed this part of my life packed away in a box with a neat bow on it, and that wasn't happening until I knew more about my mother. Minimally, her name and whether she was alive or dead. Preferably why the hell she dumped her kid and never looked back.

I had to get my butt in the shower and make myself presentable, because I was apparently doing this.

Traffic was worse than I'd planned and I had to hunt for a parking spot since the little lot that served the coffee shop was full, so I arrived with only a few minutes to spare. I'd been a little surprised that someone who worked in such a confidential business met her clients in such a public place, but then I'd realized that this was likely a screening appointment. We probably wouldn't discuss anything substantive today other than Maddie's suitability for the job and fees.

Money didn't matter. Whatever she charged, I'd pay. Hell, I'd use my mother's money to find her if I had to. The irony in that was too good not to savor. And if she was any kind of pro, this Maddie lady should be able to hook me up with another investigator if she wasn't a good fit.

When I'd asked Leila how I'd know Maddie, she'd simply instructed me to look for the woman with the red hair. It wasn't the most common of hair colors, but seriously, that was all she gave me.

I walked into the coffee shop looking for red hair. A half second later I understood why Leila's description had been so vague. I caught sight of the woman who had to be Maddie. She was hard to miss.

Flame-kissed hair that was a jumble of red and orange and blond wasn't her only striking feature.

She had flawless skin, a careless sort of style and beauty that said, "Fuck, yes, I'm hot; get over it," and skintight jeans that hugged an ass I envied.

I wasn't usually into women, but maybe I could make an exception. Except she also had an expression and sort of vibrating tension in her body that said, "I shoot first and ask questions later." Man or woman, that was too intense for me. I grinned at her, because all that bottled-up aggression was an excellent trait in an investigator I was hiring to track down my shady-as-fuck mother.

She held out her hand as I approached. I was really glad I'd gone for a sleek twist and a wrap dress rather than my usual oversized cardigan and messy bun. It gave me a confidence I might otherwise have lacked when I shook her hand. She was a little scary and a lot intimidating.

"Maddie Van Helsing. Good to meet you, Kaylee Roze."

I raised my eyebrows. I'd only provided my first name to her assistant, Leila. "Thanks for making time on such short notice."

"I was intrigued. Would you like a coffee?" When I inclined my head, she said, "They'll put it on my tab. Join me in the back corner when you're ready."

She said that like I needed a second to prepare. I

guess I did? I was about to hire this woman to find my mother. My father had held close every scrap of information, never mentioning her name, appearance, profession, how they met—nothing.

And I was about to go against his wishes to discover her identity, because...why? And why now?

Actually, the more relevant question was: why not ten years ago? Why the hell had I waited so long? It had taken me moving away from the city I'd grown up in, away from my only family, to grow the lady balls to do this.

A few minutes later, iced coffee in hand, I approached that back table like a woman on a mission. I was getting my answers.

Maddie smiled as I sat down. It was feline and a little scary. "Tell me everything."

She was perfect for this. I knew she was. So I did, starting with the trust, since it was the only lead other than the date of my birth that I had.

12

KAYLEE

I n for a penny, in for a pound.

That was the saying. I felt like hiring an investigator to find my mother was more than a penny, and resuming my morning library writing sessions was way, way more than a pound.

But close enough.

Once I'd hired Maddie it was like a dam broke. All of those childhood fears I had that I'd lose the love of the only parent I had if I wasn't "normal" enough faded a bit into the background. Hell, they should be gone. I should have outgrown that crap long ago. But since I hadn't, I'd take fading for the win.

I shouldn't still be dealing with this same old shit at thirty-one that I had at ten, but growing up with that fear had, at least in part, shaped who I was. I wasn't an idiot or completely lacking in self-awareness. I knew my overblown imagination and the way my father had handled it had made me cautious.

A kid should be assured of her father's love. Her mother's, too, for that matter. And I simply hadn't had that security as a child. Not because my dad had ever actively withheld his love. He wasn't a monster. But he could have done a little better job with his handling of a creative young girl's psyche.

I rubbed my face. Not that I really blamed him. Dad was white bread with American cheese and no crust. He couldn't truly understand the spicy grilled panini that was me. And he'd done his best to make my life easier...even though he hadn't done it in a way that in hindsight seemed all that great.

Parenting was hard stuff, and even harder as a solo gig. My dad deserved major points for showing up and trying his damnedest. Unlike the woman who'd abandoned me.

But I was at the library this morning to work. I had a book calling my name, so I shelved my crazy past and all my freaky insecurities and spent the next twenty minutes reviewing the last chapter I'd written yesterday. When I looked up, Dex was there.

I smiled slightly, then proceeded to immerse

myself in the story of Drake and his love for Kira. The irony of those names wasn't lost on me, but in my defense, I'd named Drake before I knew Dex's name. There was no excuse for Kira, especially since she was about five six, athletic but still curvy, and had dark hair with caramel highlights. Not that she was *me*; she was just a lot like me.

Surprisingly, I didn't need to ogle Dex to spark my muse this morning. Drake's story kept flowing from my weird imagination to my fingers to my laptop. And as long as that was happening, I was keeping my head down and writing. The sooner this book was done, the sooner I could get dragons out of my head and return to the safe waters of romantic suspense.

I was so wrapped up in my story that I missed Dex leaving.

No problem. In fact, that was good news. I really shouldn't be so obsessed with a guy who was involved with people who believed in magic. Because heavy baggage reasons.

I kept on writing until my stomach growled. Then I packed up and walked in the direction of my house.

Except I wasn't going home. For a change, I was going to drop by Mathilde's place unannounced.

Rather than worry over what I planned to say to her, I thought about my story. There was just something about walking and thinking that made my stories happy. No, that wasn't right, because obviously stories themselves didn't have emotions. Walking and thinking made me happier with my stories, because they tended to sort themselves out on walks.

It was one reason I opted to walk to the library instead of driving. The other was related to a need to get some of the fidgets out before sitting down to focus.

I had a treadmill in my writing shed that I used for runs, but that was an afternoon activity, once all my writing was done for the day.

Maintaining a brisk pace was actually pleasant, because the last several days had been cool. I'd heard a few Austinites mutter their thanks for the weather, so I gathered that, like Houston, Austin wasn't always so cool in the fall.

I walked, I enjoyed the weather, and I thought about my story. Right up until I knocked on Mathilde's door.

Only as my knuckles rapped firmly against her purple door did I remember that purple was the traditional color of a witch's door. And on the heels of that thought, I also realized that Dex was somewhere in the vicinity. He was her neighbor, which I'd understood to mean that he was on her street. Good thing I'd never tried to figure out what he drives, because I'd probably seen him in his car.

I kept my eyes firmly plastered to the door...for point two seconds, then I scanned the neighboring houses.

I spotted Dex's house immediately. Two doors down and easily visible from Mathilde's porch due to a curve in the road was a white brick house with black shutters and a matching front door. It had a large wraparound porch and a lot of room. The house was huge. And not huge in that McMansion way that sometimes happened in this area. No, that house was original to the neighborhood. No additions to be seen.

My own home was guilty of that sin. I didn't regret my writing shed for even an instant—and yet, I definitely had a prejudice against the houses with modern additions that just didn't fit the feel of the old, historic neighborhood.

And the worst sin of all was leveling an old home to build a more modern abode that stretched almost to the property line. Definitely not what Dex had done. His house looked even older than mine. It had probably been one of the first to go up in the neigh-borhood.

The door opened and a dirt-smudged Mathilde appeared. Her gaze followed mine. "Built on two and a half lots, circa nineteen thirty-five. He's had all the wiring redone, of course, and updated the plumbing, but the character of the place is unchanged."

Much as I appreciated it, I wasn't discussing Dex's house on Mathilde's front patio. Nevertheless, I couldn't help a tiny flare of satisfaction that I'd correctly identified Dex's home.

I squashed that emotion, turning my attention to Mathilde's uncharacteristically disheveled appear-ance. She had an actual cobweb in her hair. "Been cleaning the attic?"

She frowned and rubbed absentmindedly at her face. "In fact, yes, I have been puttering in the attic. I was looking for some reference books up there. They're stashed in boxes that are a mess. I don't suppose you could help me? I could use a bit of luck digging out the right text."

As if I was the person for that. But she was well in her eighties and didn't need to be lifting heavy boxes or crawling around in her attic all by herself. "Sure. I can help, and you can tell me all about being a love witch."

She waved a hand dismissively. "Retired love witch." When she saw the look on my face, she quickly added, "Mostly."

"Right. Not too retired to cast love spells."

She widened her eyes in a look of faux innocence. "I told you, that's just a little bit of fluff. Love spells are more of a location spell than anything else."

Before I could pursue that line of questioning, she turned down a hallway. Just as well, since I didn't really want to talk about that stupid love spell of hers. *Yet.* Because obviously I needed to ask her about it. And about her being a witch. And what connection she had to Dex and Taylor and Bain. I was pretty sure that was why my feet had taken me here.

I'd initially dismissed her talk of a love spell, primarily because I liked Mathilde and didn't want to have to consider any greater implications. *I* wasn't dabbling in fanciful magic and spells; my friend was. *I* wasn't pretending or imagining that the spell worked. My friend was.

I was perfectly well-grounded in reality.

I rolled my eyes. If I wasn't already seeing a therapist, I'd probably be telling myself I needed to see a therapist. Actually... Maybe I was due a change in that area of my life, as well. I'd moved, but I'd kept the same therapist I'd had for years in Houston. I'd ditch the virtual counseling and go with someone local. I added that to my to-do list of life changes.

"What in the world?" I muttered when I saw the ladder that Mathilde had already been up and down at least once today.

I'd only been to Mathilde's twice before, and never to the back of the house where the bedrooms were located. In the hallway, blocking our path, was a ladder pulled down from the ceiling. This was worse than I'd imagined.

"You were up there?" I asked incredulously. The ladder wasn't at all suitable for an elderly woman, no matter how nimble.

"Why do you think it took me so long to get to the front door? If I'd known you were coming, I'd have left it open for you. Come along." She looked over her shoulder. "If you're still willing to help."

She was already making her way up the rungs.

I moaned. "If you break an ankle or something, I really won't forgive you."

To her credit, Mathilde had on a pair of jeans and tennis shoes, perfect attire for the job. I hadn't noticed her unusual style choices when she'd opened the door, because of the distraction of Dex's house and the obvious dust marring her normally perfect makeup.

"I'm not going to break an ankle. Good heavens. You'd think I was a doddering cripple from the way you talk. I do adore you, darling, but that's really too much."

I refrained from replying to that comment. Besides, she'd scrambled up the ladder with the sure-footedness of a goat. Better than I was doing, actually.

"Wow. This isn't what my attic looks like at all." For one, Mathilde's was finished. Mine had studs and insulation showing.

For another, there was furniture. And shelves. Lots of shelves.

White shelves with books and plain wood shelves with jars. There were also boxes in the corner. Dust-covered and looking somewhat forlorn, and next to them was a pile of equally dusty cardboard. Deconstructed boxes, I supposed. "You've been unpacking."

"It was long overdue." Hands on her hips, she looked around the space and sighed. "I really did let this go too long. It's an absolute mess. Maybe I should tidy a bit before I dig through any more boxes?"

I examined the space. "Actually, I think we should unpack the boxes and then get rid of the cardboard. That seems to be the source of all the dust. Your attic is shockingly dust-free."

"My cleaning crew does this room along with the rest of the house, but you're right. They won't touch the boxes."

"Really? They do this room? Even though there aren't any stairs?"

She waved a hand as if that wasn't of concern. She really didn't see the problem.

"Have you thought about putting in proper stairs? It such a nice room, maybe..."

Mathilde was eyeing me with the amusement one reserves for very young children. She wasn't wrong. Stairs would be a massive renovation, and she obviously had no trouble getting up and down the ladder.

"Never mind. Let's get these unpacked." I removed my sweater and draped it over the back of one of the comfortable-looking sofa chairs. Unlike Mathilde, every day was a casual day for me. My dark jeans and black T-shirt were perfectly appropriate for this task. "Good grief. Where have you had these stored?"

While they were all neatly stacked in the corner, they were covered in dust and cobwebs.

"Right here. For the last fifty years, at least."

Fifty years. At least. I hadn't realized she'd lived in the neighborhood for quite so long.

I stopped to look at the stack of boxes. I should have noticed right away that they hadn't been moved recently. I just couldn't quite understand how they were so disgusting and the rest of the room so pristine.

It made no sense at all.

"Don't give it too much thought, dear, or you'll make your head hurt."

I frowned at her, but I didn't ask about the incongruity. She'd likely just tell me some nonsense that involved magic. "Let's unstack them and open them, then we can wash our hands and take out the contents without worrying about dirtying everything."

"An excellent plan." Mathilde removed a box cutter from her rear pocket and proceeded to slice the tape securing them closed as I set each one on the floor. I got a peek of more books and more glass jars. It seemed all the boxes held the similar contents to what was already on the shelves.

Once that was done, Mathilde smiled. "I can do

the rest myself without any trouble at all." When I protested, she shook her head. "No, I need to give the contents my full attention. I'm looking for something, and I don't want to miss it."

"If you're sure...?"

"Absolutely. Let me make you some lunch." She chuckled. "Don't give me that look. I can manage a sandwich. And I've got a clean shirt for you. You can't put your sweater over that dusty mess."

She gestured to my black T-shirt, now covered in thick stripes of dust from the boxes I'd moved.

I accepted her offer of a sandwich and a shirt, surprised when she managed to produce a T-shirt. It was made of slinky material, not the cotton of my own, and it was cut to display a hint of cleavage, but even so, it was still quite casual.

Once we were cleaned up and changed, we sat down to lunch together. I'd taken a bit longer, so when I arrived, our sandwiches were already on the table.

I stared at the grilled sandwich on my plate.

"You have a problem with paninis?" Mathilde asked, a trace of humor in her voice.

I sat down, because it was a coincidence. The spicy panini wasn't any more significant than a crustless sandwich made from white bread and American cheese would have been.

Also, I was hungry. One mouthful and oh, my, it was divine. Spicy panini for the win.

"I don't suppose you want to share some of your baggage with a friend." Mathilde had cut her sandwich into strips, making it much easier to eat.

I actually liked the messy way better, which she'd predicted. Mine was cut once diagonally. It also made for large bites. I chewed as I considered whether I wanted to discuss my reservations about involving myself, even tangentially, with things magical.

As I chewed, she said, "I didn't make a big fuss about being a witch, because I haven't practiced in years. I made a mistake some years ago, and—" She shrugged, as if it weren't of concern, but the tension in her shoulders told another tale.

I sipped the water she'd provided, stalling really. "I had an imaginary pet when I was a kid."

She lifted her eyebrows in surprise. She wasn't alone in her reaction. I hadn't actually meant to say that.

But now that I'd started... "His name was Harry, and he had purple eyes. He was about so big." I made a sphere with my hands, a little larger than a softball. "And I thought my neighbor's daughter-in-law had wings. It freaked my dad out."

"Ah." A look of sympathy—not pity—crossed her face.

And she definitely wasn't looking at me like I'd lost my marbles. Then again, Mathilde did claim to be a love witch.

"He sent me to counseling, arranged for me to switch schools when I had some problems with the other kids." I pushed away my plate. I'd eaten almost all of the sandwich and what was left was cold now anyway.

"He told you to lie."

"What? No. He just explained that the things I was seeing weren't actually there. That I had a very active imagination, and not everyone would under-stand that."

Her nostrils flared. She was angry. I thought she might say something, and I had my response at the ready. Dad was trying to do the best for me. He just wanted a normal life for me. But then she pressed her lips together and said nothing.

"So, yeah, it became a pivotal moment in my life, trying to sort out what was really there and what wasn't. Since then, I've tried to stay grounded in reality."

"Except for your books."

"Well, yes, but that's fiction, and I don't really write books with fantasy elements." Drake lurked in my head, mocking those words. "Usually."

She raised her eyebrows. "You've strayed from sexy police officers and former special ops men with bulging muscles?"

Mathilde knew all of my Kitty Sweet secrets, so why not this one?

I covered my eyes. "Were-dragons. Feel free to mock. Go right ahead, because I'm probably already thinking it."

"Oh, my." That wasn't a mocking tone.

I looked up to find hearts in Mathilde's eyes and her hands clasped to her chest.

"What? What are you thinking?"

A little breathy sigh escaped before she said, "Dragons." Then her eyes lost the dreamy look. "Not that I'll ever admit it."

"Ah...you'll never admit your love of were-dragon romance? I promise not to tell." Tentacle porn was a thing. Pretty sure Mathilde's interest in hunky dragons wasn't going to shock anyone. But to each their own, and I wasn't about to kink shame anyone...even for being ashamed of their kink.

"Technically, darling, dragons wouldn't be weres,

would they? Because weres are bitten; shifters are born."

"Okay, except you know that every author has their own rules, right?"

She sat up and clasped her hands. It was incongruously schoolmarmish. "Be that as it may, dragons are shifters, not weres." She blinked. "In my head. That's how I see them."

Weirder and weirder.

"Got it. I'll keep that in mind." When she smiled, I added, "But I'm not even sure I'll publish this one. I just need to get the story written and out of my head, so I can move on to my next real project."

Something about that—just get it done and out of my head—resonated. Maybe I just needed to get a certain nerdy-hot guy "done and out of my head."

I'd thought it before. More as advice my writer friends would give me, but still...

"Whatever you say." Her expression was pleasant enough, her words minimally neutral, and even her tone was agreeable—but she thought I was talking out of my ass. She might not be wrong.

"Ugh, don't tell me you think I'm going to pivot to dragon romance. This is supposed to be a one-off." I suddenly recalled Taylor's fixation on dragon sex. Google hadn't been helpful. "Hey, what do you know about dragon sex? Uh, not in the context of romance books."

Her lips twitched. "Taylor's been talking, I presume."

"Yeah, she's a little out there." I didn't get into the whole "she totally believes you're a witch and you really cast a love spell" thing. "She says she's a little psychic."

"Hmm. What do you think about that?"

"Seriously, Mathilde? What am I supposed to say? You're a love witch. She's a psychic. I just don't believe in the same things that y'all do."

"So you don't believe that Taylor is psychic." Her lack of concern was...interesting.

"No." Implied was that I also didn't believe that she was a love witch. But we'd had that conversation. Not about her being a witch, but about her faith in spells that I simply couldn't believe in.

"But you liked her." She grinned.

I rolled my eyes. "Yes, she's very likeable, even drunk, but..."

"You don't want to be friends with someone who's walking on the weird side."

Those words coming from the mouth of a woman who was equally weird, but whose friendship I wasn't willing to abandon hit home. "You think I should give her a chance."

"I think she's a lovely girl. *Woman*," she corrected. "And I think she would benefit from the friendship of a kind soul."

I smirked. "And that's me, huh?" I hadn't ever considered myself especially kind. Sometimes people took shy and quiet as "nice." I wasn't evil. I was a decent person, but I also was no Mother Teresa.

"You have a beautiful soul." Her smile was sad. "I wish you saw that in yourself."

"No need, when I have people like you to tell me how great I am." But I didn't have many people like Mathilde in my life, and she was the only one who actually lived in the same city as me. "I'll think about giving her a call."

"You do what you think is best."

And on that, we parted ways. Mathilde promised to call when she was ready to resume our standing lunch appointment. "I'm going to be busy," she explained. "Sorting out those boxes."

"That's right. You said you were looking for something."

She nodded, but didn't explain what had gone missing. Then again, it had to be something to do with her witch life, because I'd realized at some point that her attic was a witch's den. Kind of cool in the abstract, but less exciting in reality since it was a reminder of the fundamental differences in our beliefs.

Only after the door closed behind me did I remember she hadn't followed up on the dragon sex thing. I'd just have to ask one of my online writer friends.

Standing on my friend's porch, I took a deep breath and looked at the house two doors down.

I'd hired an investigator to find my mother, and I wasn't terrified that my father would never speak to me again.

I'd reaffirmed a friendship with a woman I knew was an actively practicing witch. Heck, I'd helped her start unpacking what was likely the contents of her witchy cupboard and spell book library. And I wasn't suddenly seeing imaginary animals or wings or sparkly people.

Heck, I was considering giving Taylor a call, because she hadn't done anything wrong, and I liked her. It wasn't like I'd be guilty by association. *She* wasn't guilty, not of anything but believing things I didn't believe in. And why was that such a terrible thing?

My dad and even my therapist had conditioned me to believe that I had to tightly control my environment and be cautious of the people I allowed close. That I needed to stay grounded in reality.

These people were all very real, and I *liked* them. It was past time I moved a little outside my comfort zone.

I marched across the street, hands sweating. Mostly because I was also thinking about that whole fuck-him-out-of-my-system plan. It was a solid plan. Once Dex wasn't in my head, maybe Drake would let me wrap up my book—and I wouldn't end up writing an entire new series about were-dragons.

I wiped my hands on my jeans. Knocking on a man's door was no big deal. Just because I didn't know a lot about him other than I was crazy attracted to him, and his friends fell in the kooky range, that didn't make propositioning him any big deal. He obviously was into me physically, and the only reason I'd turned him down initially was because I told myself I wasn't up for a pump-and-dump situation. But this wouldn't be that, because I'd be the one using his smoking hot body and then walking away.

I rapped firmly on the door three times. I didn't even know if he'd be in. He probably wasn't.

He was in.

Definite yes.

I inhaled when the door opened, revealing muscles. Sweat-dampened, glorious muscles.

At first, all I could see was a landscape of gorgeous chest. But then my eyes swept his body for closer detail, because how could I not look? From his biceps to his pecs to the ridges in his abdomen, the man was perfection.

I was lingering on the V his low-riding athletic shorts revealed, when Dex's amused voice registered.

"I thought you weren't speaking to me."

13

DEX

Kaylee had practically ignored me at the library. One tentative smile and then nothing. No covert looks from under her lashes, no sneaky glances at my ass when I retrieved a new book. My stalker wasn't stalking me.

But she hadn't avoided the place entirely, and that in itself was a win.

A small one in comparison to *this*. Arriving on my doorstep when I hadn't even given her my phone number, let alone my address—definitely a win.

I let her get a good look. I'd just come home from a run with Chelsea a few minutes ago and was about to hop in the shower when I heard the knock. The appreciative look in Kaylee's eyes told me exactly what she thought of my shirtless, sweaty state.

After she'd traced my abs, I decided it was probably better not to scare her with the monster in my shorts. That happened when a hot woman checked me out. Actually, not usually, but it obviously happened when *Kaylee* checked me out. Her gaze was almost perceptible. A ghost of a touch on my skin.

I cleared my throat. "I thought you weren't speaking to me."

She gulped. Audibly. It was adorable. And also, fuck, if she was that turned on by my half-naked body, then how would she react to me stripped nude and hard for her?

I could do that. I was more than halfway there in both respects.

Her gaze jerked up to meet mine, and she flushed. Then she frowned. "What? Why would you think that?" But then the frown cleared. "Oh, no. I was just writing."

And then she blushed again.

What was she typing away on her computer that made her turn so deliciously pink?

But more important than that, she hadn't been ignoring me. She'd been busy.

"You can wipe that self-satisfied smirk off your face."

I grinned wider. "I don't think so. And I'm not self-satisfied. I'm pleased. It makes me happy that you aren't ignoring me after I set you up on a friend date with my best friend's crazy...ah, girlfriend. It obviously didn't end well."

"Why did you do that? She didn't exactly sing your praises." She crossed her arms, which made her tits look fabulous. Even the ugly sweaters she liked to wear couldn't hide their sweet curve.

She must have ten of those grandma sweaters. So far I'd seen black, beige, dark blue, dark purple, and some kind of pinky purple color. Today's was a deep forest green...that framed her surprisingly lush tits. It didn't hurt that she had a clingy navy T-shirt on underneath that had a V neck. Her shirt dipped just enough to give a hint of cleavage when she pushed her breasts together like she was now.

Not that she realized what she was doing. For such a smoking babe, she was pretty damn oblivious of her fire.

When I'd fully mastered a look that let me stare at her breasts while seeming to look at her face, I said, "Full disclosure, I hoped she'd say a few nice things about me, but she has a...I don't know, not a grudge, but a bias against me, because I retrieved her keys from her purse when she was wasted one night."

She stared at me, like she was trying to crack a criminal mastermind under interrogation lights. "I don't get it."

"Me either. Something about violating the sanctity of her purse."

"No, still don't get it, but it does sound like something Taylor would say. If you weren't sure she'd pimp you, why did you send her to the library?"

"I thought you two might like each other." And I'd been wrong. I wasn't infallible, though I usually had good instincts about that shit.

"We did. We *do*."

This had the ring of an "it's complicated" explanation. Before she could explain, I opened the door wider. "Do you want to come inside?"

This time when she took in my partially clothed self, she made it below my waist. I was only partially hard at this point. Talking about my buddy's mate had a deflating effect.

But the bulge was still noticeable, and her eyes got big.

Gaze firmly fixed on my shorts, she said, "I'm interrupting you. I don't want to..."

And then she licked her lips.

Fuck.

Whatever she didn't want to do was lost. She just stopped and stared.

At my dick.

My voice a little rough—but who could blame me? I had visions of Kaylee licking me like a lollipop going through my head—I said, "Please. Come inside."

Then I stepped back.

It was like there was a string between my dick and her eyes, because as I stepped back she moved forward, never taking her eyes off the almost full-blown monster now residing in my shorts.

I had a choice here. Push my advantage and probably have incredibly hot sex with my stalker—my dick was firmly on board with this choice—or find out why she was at my house. It was a mystery considering her brunch with Taylor went awry, she'd refused a ride home with me even though she obviously knew we were neighbors, she'd skipped out on the library for a few days, and when she'd come back today, she'd mostly ignored me.

I knew what the right choice was, but it was also the one where I didn't get laid in the next five minutes, so it took me a second to gather my resolve. My dick didn't make my decisions, but damn, it was difficult to naysay the dude when Kaylee looked like she was ready to devour me.

"Can I get you a coffee? Or water?" I hated asking, but I knew it was the right thing to do.

She seemed to be weighing her options. Maybe she was a tea drinker.

"We're having sex." She announced it like she expected an argument.

Which was pretty fucking funny. Also, it looked like it hadn't been tea that was on her mind.

"Okay."

She blinked. "Right now." Then she blinked again. "I mean, if you want to have sex?"

"Oh, I definitely want that." I took her hand and pulled her close. "But—"

She groaned, one hand pressed against my chest. "Don't tell me you want to talk first."

How was this happening? How was I the one wanting to talk and she was the one wanting to fuck my brains out? Fate really was laughing at my ass right now.

I was still holding her hand, but the other one, the one she'd pressed against my chest, was wandering, massaging my pecs. Her thumb brushed my nipple, and I flinched.

I trapped her roaming hand underneath mine. "Give me five minutes, then—

Her lips touched my chest. Then found a nipple. Her teeth gently scraped, and my hips thrust forward...into her hand.

Fuck me. Kaylee had her hand down my shorts. Then she wrapped her fingers around my cock and shoved my shorts down. I couldn't help but look down.

I'd never noticed her dark, sparkly nail polish before, or how small her hands were. Fuck.

"We can talk after." She gave me a tug to emphasize her point.

When a woman had my junk in her hand—no, when Kaylee had my cock in her hand—I wasn't about to argue with anything that came out of her mouth. I sure as fuck wasn't going to argue for us not to have sex.

"You're sure about this?" I had to ask. Confirmation wasn't arguing. She'd mildly stalked me, then turned me down for a date, then placed herself firmly on the other side of the fence when she'd discovered I kept company with a bunch of kooky, magic-believers.

She'd been all over the place signal-wise...not that there was any ambiguity in the kisses she was peppering across my chest. And even less so with her hand working my cock like she was on a mission to make me come.

She kissed then tongued my left nipple. Looking up at me with her passion-hazed brown eyes, I was pretty sure I'd make Bain, the grumpy fucker, look like a cheerful sprite if she said she'd changed her mind. "I want you."

I inhaled deeply.

But just in case that wasn't enough, she said, "I want to have sex with you."

Hmm. I could have just gone with the wanting me part. Sex was good. Given the fact my balls were drawn up tight against my body and my cock was so hard it hurt, sex was better than good.

But it was pretty clear that Kaylee *only* wanted to have sex.

What the fuck was wrong with me? Like that had ever stopped me before? I preferred women who weren't clingers.

Once I'd wrapped my head around the idea that sex was good, great even, I said, "Bedroom?"

"Hell yes."

So I picked her up.

About ten feet from my bedroom door, Kaylee's entire body tensed. "Do you have a *baby*?"

She sounded appalled, which was confusing on so many levels. Why were we talking about babies? And why were babies terrible? Babies were cute.

I blamed the fact that my brain was oxygen deprived since almost all of the blood flow in my body was located further south. That was why it took me so long to figure out the problem. "Oh, hell."

I set Kaylee on the ground. She wobbled so I kept my arm wrapped around her as I gave my dog a talking to. "Chels, hush."

The whimpers that might sound vaguely child-like to a woman who had no clue I lived with a dog stopped.

Snuggling Kaylee against my side, I nuzzled her neck. "No baby, just a roommate. You're not scared of dogs, are you?"

She went limp, obviously relieved that I wasn't hiding a secret baby in my bedroom. Which was a bizarre assumption to make, but then—we didn't know each other very well.

"I don't have a girlfriend, a wife, or an ex-wife. I have no kids, just a dog. Can I?" I indicated the door.

"Oh, yes. Please. Definitely. I like dogs."

Except I wasn't so sure that she did. When I opened the door, Chelsea nudged it with her nose, flinging it open. The door banged loudly against the bedroom wall.

Chelsea had a great sense of smell, so she'd already known I had a visitor. Hence all the excited noises she'd made and that Kaylee had misheard as a baby's cry. She was pretty polite, so she stood, tail flagged out behind her and wagging, waiting for Kaylee to deliver the pets and praise she was accustomed to.

But Kaylee took one look at Chelsea and tensed again.

Worse, she started to breathe fast, like she was hyperventilating.

No, she was hyperventilating.

"Chelsea, bed." I pointed to my bedroom.

With sad eyes and a droopy tail, she turned back around and planted herself on the dog bed in my room.

Once I had the bedroom door closed, I wrapped my arm around Kaylee again and rubbed her back. "What can I do?"

She shook her head, but there was a shine in her eyes that predicted tears.

"Oh, hell. I'm sorry. She looks scary, but she's a sweetheart. I swear." There were a few people who'd been frightened by Chelsea—she was a breed known for protection and bite work—but not anything like this. Chels was so obviously sweet and friendly that most people got over it pretty fast.

Kaylee just shook her head.

Well, this sucked. I loved my dog, and the woman I had the hots for was terrified of her.

But that was a problem for later—when Kaylee wasn't looking so pale. She looked terrible. Her natural skin tone was warm, like she spent a lot of time in the sun, so the pallor she was currently exhibiting looked especially sickly.

I kept rubbing her back and started to inch her away from the bedroom. She shot a glance over her shoulder, and her eyes got even brighter.

Fuck this. I picked her up and cuddled her against my chest. Once we were in the living room, I set her down on the sofa. "What can I do?"

She sat on the sofa, head between her legs. "Nothing. I'll be fine in a second."

She was lying. I could hear it in her voice.

She slowly got her color back, and then she said she thought it best if she left.

And she did.

I'd been debating talking over sex, and in the end, we did neither. What the hell had just happened?

14

KAYLEE

Dex's dog glowed.

As I clutched my fluffy sweater tighter around me, I thought about calling my therapist, but I just...I couldn't. I knew what would happen. She'd want me to consider whether I should go back to Houston. That wasn't happening. She'd want me to consider whether medication was a good option, but I didn't want to take psych drugs. No way.

It wasn't like I saw that glow and thought it was normal or real. I knew it wasn't. I didn't need drugs.

I just needed Dex's dog not to glow.

My backpack felt like it weighed a ton. Everything was heavy. Even walking was hard. But my need to be home in my own space, where nothing glowed and everything was familiar, propelled me forward.

It had been just like this when I was a kid. When I wasn't really paying attention, I'd catch the light out of the corner of my eye. I'd turn, and there it would be: a neighbor's daughter-in-law with wings, the first time I'd seen Harry, the man down the street with the wolf eyes who'd always looked hungry. Honestly, there were too many instances to recount.

This time, I'd been distracted by lust. Almost all of my attention had been on Dex. I was relieved that he didn't have a crib set up next to his bed, because how weird would that be? Guys with babies didn't live alone and disappear to the library for hours on end. They had wives and talked about their children and showed people baby pictures.

Come to think about it, most guys didn't hang out at the library all morning, because they had jobs. I'd never even thought about that. What did Dex do for a living?

But it didn't matter anymore, because he had a dog that glowed. Not really. Obviously. But I couldn't spend time with a man who had a dog that I *thought* glowed.

Oh. My. God. What if my dad had been right?

Maybe I wasn't ready for this move? What if I was as fragile as he believed me to be?

What the fuck?

I didn't *feel* fragile. I felt *angry*. And confused. Betrayed, but I wasn't sure by whom.

And I'd been so sure that striking out completely on my own was the right choice. Right up until now. I may have had doubts with a little "d" but now I had big D Doubts.

My phone rang as I reached my house. I dug it out of my backpack in time to see that it was Maddie Van Helsing, then it rolled over to voicemail.

She must either need me to authorize more funds or she had some additional questions for me, because it had only been a day. She couldn't have anything useful for me in such a short period of time.

I waited to listen to the voicemail until I was home and had a cup of tea in front of me.

It wasn't long, and she wasn't asking for anything.

"I found your mother. Let me know when you want to meet... Maybe your house."

And that was it.

Her tone had been neutral. The only telling moment was the brief hesitation before she'd mentioned my place. Maybe it was bad news. Maybe my mother was dead, and she wanted me to be able to bawl in privacy.

I didn't know, and I wasn't gonna find out. Not right this second. I couldn't deal with her and her news right now.

Normally, I'd lose myself in a book to escape the stress of my life, but that wasn't an option. I was too wrapped up in the story I was creating to enjoy someone else's words. Which left me hanging in the wind.

I did a quick recap of my recent life choices. Specifically the ones that had put me in situations that had triggered my childhood imaginings again.

First, I was driven to write a story with magic.

Then my neighbor and closest friend in town casts a love spell for me.

Then I have lunch with a psychic.

And now I'm seeing glowing dogs.

One glowing dog.

Still.

Fucking hell, how was this my life? When all I wanted was to move to a new town, start my own life, be independent and happy, and do the job I loved. Maybe make some friends who were like me, spicy panini people.

Speaking of spicy paninis... I liked Mathilde. More than liked. I cared about her. And I liked Taylor.

And how could l not like Dex? Smoking hot and so incredibly sweet. The guy tried to find me a friend. Sure, that meant I seemed like a lost, lonely, sad soul in need of help finding friends—but since I was at least some of those things, I couldn't really be upset that he'd spotted it and tried to help. While also furthering his own cause, but still...Taylor was hardly the person best suited to that purpose. She had, however, been quite well-suited as a potential friend to me. And it was hard to find people open to new friendships, especially working from home like she and I both did.

I sighed, because Dex's attributes didn't end there. I'd thrown myself at him, and while sporting literally the largest hard-on I'd ever seen in my life, he asked me if I was sure. Not because he didn't want me. I was sure he did. No, he'd slowed it down to be sure that *I* was sure.

And then I'd freaked out, and all he'd cared about was making everything okay for me.

I groaned and let my head fall to the kitchen table. There wasn't enough tea or enough warm sweaters in the world to make this better.

He was the perfect guy.

I wanted him like crazy.

And I couldn't have him because of the fucking glowing dog.

And the worst part? I didn't just want to sleep with him and get him out of my system. Every time I talked to him, touched him, I wanted him more, not less. And no way was having awesome sex with him going to make that disappear.

I did the only thing I could think of to distract myself. I changed into workout clothes and hopped on the treadmill.

Spoiler: it didn't work. My body was occupied, but my mind was still stuck on the same problems. The same confusions. The same worries.

But at least I wore myself out enough to get a decent night's sleep.

Maddie and her revelations could wait till tomorrow.

I should have crashed hard. That was the kind of physical, deep-muscle tired that I'd achieved yesterday.

I'd spent twice as long on the treadmill as usual and then taken a hot shower afterwards. Lots of water and a long pour of red wine later, and I had every right to expect to awake refreshed.

Instead, I woke with the smell of a certain nerdy-hot guy in my nose. Hell, in my *lungs*. Like I'd huffed vanilla and sugar all night long.

Images from the night flashed through my head. Scents. Touches. It had been so real.

With my arm over my eyes to block out the light, I revisited the feel of his muscular chest and broad shoulders under my palms, the shockingly soft brush of his beard on my thighs, the delicate touch of his fingers as he touched me, stroked, rubbed... His tongue as he lapped at my entrance, then my clit...

I reached between my legs. I was so close. That I could be on the edge of orgasm without any physical stimulation... Whatever. I'd think about that after I rubbed one out.

I was drenched, my panties nowhere to be found. I dipped two fingers inside, but I still felt an empty ache.

Frustrated, I moved my fingers to my clit, picturing the bulge in Dex's shorts. Imagining him pulling down those shorts, the smack of his hard cock against his abs, the warmth of his huge body over mine.

The feel of him, thick and hard at my entrance. The stretch as he filled me, as he fucked me. Hips thrusting, grinding against my clit, harder and—

"Ohmygod, Dex! Yes!"

Several seconds—minutes?—later, I opened my eyes. I'd just come so hard, I'd blacked out. There was a good imagination, and there was seeing stars. I'd never even done that with a flesh-and-blood man, and yet imaginary Dex had managed it without laying a finger on me. I blamed it on his fictional mouth. Or his hands. No, really it was his cock.

Dream Dex had a really, really nice dick.

I snorted, remembering the size of Dex's bulge in his athletic shorts. Because, damn. It had been so sexy, the image had imprinted on my brain. But the crazy part was that I'd apparently done some math while sleeping and extrapolated the size of his dick from that glimpse. Worse, I was pretty sure I'd come close on the girth and length. How obsessed was I that I could do that in my sleep?

I snorted again, because—who wouldn't be obsessed? He was nerdy-hot, built, nice, kind, thoughtful, and in my dream gave amazing oral.

Damn, I'd needed that. Not the oral, the orgasm.

I laid in bed, half-comatose from the endorphins and whatever sex hormones made people happy as hell and just drifted. Not quite asleep, just insanely relaxed.

My postorgasmic euphoria was cut short by the jarring ring of my phone. Whoever was calling me at early o'clock and killing my buzz was a dead person.

When I retrieved my phone, I realized it was later than I'd thought. By a lot. I'd slept through my seven-thirty alarm by over two hours. No wonder it was blindingly bright in my room.

I rejected the call, recognizing only after hitting the red icon on my cell that it was Maddie Van Helsing. Damn. The name alone brought everything back: she had news, but I didn't give two fucks because I was seeing glowing shit out in the world again.

Thanks for that dose of reality, lady. Not that I blamed her. I was paying the woman, and I wasn't so absorbed in my own drama that I didn't realize she had a job to do. I rubbed my face, then texted back my apologies and offered to meet her at my house after lunch.

Once she'd confirmed and I'd provided my address, I checked my other texts. One from Mathilde asking if perhaps I'd stopped by to see a certain handsome neighbor on my way home, a second to say that she guessed not since that handsome neighbor was in a foul temper, and a final one saying that I should text her back before she showed up at my house with a crowbar to make sure I was still alive.

I chuckled, because I'd bet she actually would. Hopefully, the crowbar was to open the front door and not to beat some sense into me.

And this was why I didn't care that she was a witch—love-spell-casting or otherwise—because I cared about her and she cared about me. Mathilde was good people.

I sent off a quick text explaining I'd overslept but was fine. Then asked if we could skip lunch today and do dinner instead. I added: *I might have news.*

Then I took a breath to steady my nerves. The other text I had was from an unknown number, but I could guess from the preview that it was Dex.

I got your number from Mathilde. You can be mad later, but please tell me you're okay first. I didn't want to knock on your door, because that would be weird. Right? But I was worried about you. You weren't yourself when you left.

Oh, Dex. I was myself. My neurotic, worried, stressed-out self.

He didn't seem scared by the brief glimpse he'd gotten behind my curtain. Pretty damn crazy given how completely chill he always appeared to be. In my experience, anyone with that much chill worked at it. Most especially by excluding all of the not-chill people from their inner circle.

I'd been feeling a bit adrift since moving to Austin. My dad and I used to get together for monthly dinners at my place, but more than that, I had local writer friends, and my routines and habits were long-established. My life in Houston had been like a well-worn robe. Comfy and familiar and shaped just right to my body.

I'd had a rough few days, and now I had two people wanting to know that I was all right. For the first time, Austin didn't feel so cold.

This house was my comfy little haven. I'd settled into it like the nesting homebody I was and claimed it MINE. But the city had been a place I lived—until now. Now it was at least starting to become mine as well.

I drafted a text and then erased it and then drafted another and erased it as well. The first said too much, the second not enough. I finally sent: *I'm not mad. Thanks for checking in with me. It's kind of a long story, but I'm not afraid of your dog.*

After I sent it, I sent a second: *I'm okay.*

I even added a smile emoji. Go me! Spoiler: I wasn't feeling smiley.

Warmer from the inside out. More welcome. Less alone.

Not smiley.

His reply was bizarre and sweet and completely pushy.

I'm bringing soup.

A second passed and he sent another.

I'll leave it on your doorstep.

And then a few seconds later:

It's Thai coconut curry. No one can say no to Thai coconut curry soup.

When another text didn't appear, I stopped staring at my phone.

He wanted to feed me. That seemed...significant?

My phone pinged again with another text, and my heart thudded erratically in my chest. But when I looked, I saw that it was Mathilde replying to my earlier dinner invitation and comment about news.

I'm in. Six o'clock? And that news, I'm guessing it's about your mother. Let me know whether I'm bringing champagne or vodka.

I agreed to the time and refrained from comment regarding the drinks. I'd have to get back to her on that one, though it was hard to imagine a scenario that involved bubbly.

I hopped in the shower, a necessity given my intermittent sleep the night previous, then—and this was truly shocking given my plans for the day—I wrote for a few hours.

Maybe because I couldn't do anything about Maddie's news, not until she gave it to me.

Maybe because I'd been inspired by my morning jill-off session.

Maybe because the story had been building in the back of my head and just needed out.

Whatever the reason, I flew through a scene and a half of Drake's book. I also made a change. My were-dragons became shifters.

I was deep in the midst when my phone pinged. I usually silenced it, or better yet, didn't even bring it out to my writing shed, but given everything that was going on, it seemed smart to keep it handy.

Soup's on the porch.

That was it. I waited a few seconds to be sure, but that was the only text.

With a glance to confirm that it was indeed time for lunch—twelve on the dot—I saved my manuscript file, closed my laptop, and headed for my waiting soup.

Except it wasn't just soup. There was also a square ceramic casserole dish with one of those reusable silicone stretchy things over the top. Whatever it was, it was clearly homemade. The soup was store bought. A brand I recognized, but there was no doubt about the other item. I peered closer and could just make out what looked like cocoa powder through the clear silicone. Unless Dex had kitchen fairies, he'd *baked* for me.

My phone, still in my hand, pinged with a text.

I thought you might like a "pick me up" so I left you some tiramisu.

I didn't speak Italian, but wild guess that was the meaning of tiramisu. Which made sense, since it was made with coffee. Homemade tiramisu. That seemed like kind of a big deal.

I looked up from my crouched position on my porch to find a large, handsome, bearded man in the street in front of my neighbor's house. Not looming, but making sure I got my delivery. He waved.

I couldn't help the grin that spread across my face. In part because he was just so damn handsome and his sheepish expression made him even more so, but also because it looked like I'd gained a stalker.

Aka a concerned friend.

Who didn't want to pressure me by pounding on my door when I was stressed out.

Who did want to fuck me with his very large cock.

And also feed me soup and bake me tiramisu.

How could that not make me grin?

THE SMILE that I'd worn all through lunch and that had lurked, waiting to break through even after Maddie arrived and planted herself at my kitchen table, faded to nothing more than a memory when she announced, "I found your mother."

Yeah, I knew that was coming. She'd warned me in her voicemail when she'd requested the meeting. And I hadn't forgotten. I'd just, sort of, not focused on it. I wanted to know. I didn't want to know. I went back and forth. But the important point was that I *needed* to know. In order to move on with my life, I needed to know that I'd made an effort to put my mother and her abandonment behind me—but that took some work on my part.

This was me, doing that work.

"She's alive?" Because obviously she was, or Maddie would have said something along the lines of: *I have bad news for you. I found your mother, but she's passed away.*

Actually, I hadn't known Maddie long, but I suspected it would be more along the lines of: *Your mom's dead.*

Maddie eyed me like I had a contagious disease.

I rolled my eyes. "I'm not going to freak out."

She huffed out an annoyed breath. "You say that now."

When she didn't clarify, I said, "So? What did you find? And how the hell did you manage to come up with something so quickly?"

"She wasn't hiding." She tapped the table nervously. No, it wasn't nerves. More like excess energy. "So, here's the thing. You need to have a talk with your father."

"Right, except I'm paying you, because my father won't tell me shit." All the swears I usually saved for my books and my thoughts were coming out.

Maybe it was her ripped jeans and combat boots. Maybe her expression. Maddie just seemed like a person who could handle all the swears.

"And I'm going to give you all the information I have exactly for that reason. I'm just warning you that you won't believe me, and you'll need to call your father for verification."

This time I contained my eye roll, but seriously, what was up with her? It was like I had FRAGILE LITTLE WOMAN stamped on my fucking head. "I'm not fragile."

Her eyes widened, and she laughed. "Yeah, no shit."

She still didn't say anything. She was obviously stalling.

She'd refused a drink earlier, but this time I

offered something better. "Do you want some tiramisu? A, ah, friend just dropped some off, home-made. I haven't tried it yet, but I bet it's good."

Not because I actually knew whether Dex was a decent baker; more because Dex seemed like the kind of guy who did everything well.

She perked up and stopped fidgeting. "Hell, yes. And I'll take that coffee if you're still offering. With cream, if you have it."

I plated two servings on my good dishes as I waited for the water to boil, then retrieved forks and cloth napkins.

As I puttered in the kitchen, waiting for the coffee to brew, I filled the silence with idle questions. "Have you been a PI for long?"

"A while. I've never done anything else." Her hand fluttered above her midsection for the briefest of moments before she said, "I'm trying to take more cases like yours now."

"Cases like mine? Digging up dirt on families?"

"Ah, no. Not in particular. Just more investigative work. Less hands-on field work."

What kind of hands-on field work did a PI do? Maddie was tall and she looked really fit. I'd bet she was wicked fast if all that nervous energy of hers was anything to go by, but really, what would fieldwork entail? Personal protection, maybe?

I didn't ask, because that went beyond small talk. Especially bringing up the telling gesture she'd made. My bet was that Maddie was pregnant. She wore a broad wedding band, no gems. Almost like something a man would wear, but it was delicately etched with symbols or leaves or flowers. I hadn't been able to make out the detail without staring.

The timer dinged, saving me from further chitchat.

I delivered our coffee—again opting for my good china—and then sat down. Neither of us said a word, instead choosing to focus on our dessert.

My reason was clear. I was ready to judge Dex based on his baking skills. Unfair? Yes. But I was going to nonetheless. Not that there was a bad outcome possible. If it wasn't good, then it wasn't something he made often, which meant he'd gone to extra trouble just for me. If it was good, that didn't minimize the trouble he'd gone to, but it possibly explained why the man smelled like baked goods all the damn time. Too edible, by far. He was walking temptation—for so many reasons.

"You're staring at that like it might bite you." I

looked up to find Maddie's amused gaze on me. "In case you're wondering, it's fucking amazing."

A third of hers was already gone.

She shrugged. "I like sweets."

I took a bite, and holy hell, it was amaaaazing. My nanna, my dad's mother who'd passed when I was a kid, used to say that desserts made with love tasted the best. If that was true, then there was a fuck-ton of love in this.

"Right?" Maddie said, giving me a knowing look as I dove for a second bite.

We finished our tiramisu in silence, both of us appreciating the beauty of the perfectly prepared creamy, cakey, coffee-saturated heaven that was before us.

When her plate was practically licked clean, Maddie asked, "Who's this friend? You should put him or her on retainer as your personal chef."

Which sparked some naughty thoughts that didn't belong at my kitchen table, especially as I sat across from the woman who was about to break incredibly bad news if her behavior thus far was any indication.

She smirked. "Hope he or she is as good in bed as they are in the kitchen."

I shoved any thoughts of Dex far, far away...even if I wondered the same thing. "My mother?"

"Ah." She pushed her plate away. "She's a demon. She left you with your father after you were born with the understanding that if you showed any signs of possessing magic, he was to immediately contact her so you could be properly trained."

I stared at her, because...a demon?

Then I blushed. Not because *I* was embarrassed. Or rather, I was, but only on behalf of Maddie. I should have suspected this would be a possibility, since she'd been recommended by Mathilde, who claimed to be a witch. But even if Maddie believed in the same things that Mathilde did, that didn't explain why she'd make up some BS about my mother belonging to their witches and demons club.

Maddie sighed. "I fucking hate these conversations." She clasped her hands together on the table. "There are the magical and the nonmagical. Sometimes the two intersect, fuck like rabbits, and have offspring. That offspring can have no magic, some magic, or a lot of magic. You're the latter. When the magical part of the procreation equation is a demon and the child has a lot of magic, you get a witch. Which is what you are."

I'd gone from flushed to chilled as she spoke.

She seemed so...certain. So assured in her perceptions. It reminded me of myself when I was younger, believing in all the things that could not be. Her conviction scared me.

She unclasped her hands and leaned forward a bit. "Also, I'm not a PI. I'm a monster hunter. The magical who hurt humans are considered monsters —and disposable. So heads up, don't become a serial-killing witch or I will come for your ass."

I'm not sure why it was the threat to my very existence that pushed me over the edge, but that did it. I snorted. It was a sort of hysterical laugh held back but not entirely.

I tried to keep my expression as passive as possible, but I covered my mouth just in case I couldn't quite manage it.

Laughing at the woman who'd just threatened my life, however circuitously, didn't seem wise. Even if my mirth was of the hysterical variety.

The worst part was that I wasn't just laughing outright. My response was grounded in an excess of emotion that was part panic and part fear. Kind of the definition of hysteria.

And why was that? I asked myself.

The answer was horrifying.

Part of me believed her.

Maddie sighed. "Call your father. I'd think anyone saying this was nuts, too, if I'd lived your life."

I couldn't help asking, even though the answer was obvious. "You really believe in all this? Magic, monsters, demons, witches?"

There was pity in her eyes. Or maybe sympathy. It was hard to tell. "I was raised in the midst of it. Finding a witch's demon mother is one of the tamer assignments I've had lately."

The panic in my chest was easing, probably due to the fact that I couldn't sit at my kitchen table, petrified, after having shared the best tiramisu of my life with a woman who seemed for the most part pretty damn down to earth.

For a second, I was tempted to ask what else had come across her proverbial desk, but really—why bother when I (mostly) wouldn't believe her anyway?

"Call your dad." She sighed. "He owes you a dose of reality. You deserve that."

I was allowed to be annoyed with my father, but she had no right.

"Glare all you want. It's clear you've been suppressing your magic for a while now. That's not healthy, and it sure as fuck isn't safe. For you or the people around you. How are you supposed to know what you can do if you don't have any training? Any practice? Any supervision?"

I shook my head. Because... No. That wasn't my reality.

"A word of warning. Mommy Dearest isn't the warm fuzzy sort of demon. She made a deal with your dad, and he broke faith by keeping your magic a secret. You don't want her pissed, and he *really* doesn't."

"Are you telling me that the woman I had you find is a danger to my father?" That seemed more real than anything else she'd said so far.

"Quite possibly. Call your dad." She pushed her chair back and was standing. "And after you call him —" She pulled a business card from her pocket and placed it on the table. It had a name—a woman's name—and a number, nothing else.

I had to ask. I felt foolish, but—"Ah, what kind of..." I closed my eyes, because the words had to be spoken aloud or I'd smack myself later, however idiotic I felt voicing them. Fuck it. "What kind of demon is my mother supposed to be?"

"The war kind." She patted my shoulder on the way out.

KAYLEE

I cancelled dinner with Mathilde.

And lunch.

For a week.

I also did not call my dad.

I definitely didn't call the woman whose name was on the card: Lizbet Jones. My mother. Supposedly.

Definitely the woman who'd funded the trust set up for my benefit. Definitely the woman who claimed to have given birth to me, if Maddie was to be believed.

Because Maddie Van Helsing sent me a report in which she outlined the money trail she'd followed and the interview she'd held with the person who'd pulled the strings to create my trust.

It was a lot of money, so it seemed a little insane that whoever set it up *wasn't* my biological mother.

I went round and round in circles for several days. I had a little time to dither and fret and wonder at my sanity, at least in regards to anticipated repercussions from a livid war demon. Maddie had texted me that same evening after she left and assured me that my alleged mother didn't as yet know that I (her daughter, maybe?) was in possession of magic (ha!), contrary to my father's assurances to the contrary. So long as that remained true, I needn't fear reprisal against my father.

If Maddie was to be believed, then I had magic, my mom was a war demon, and if, or rather when, Mommy Dearest found out about my magic, my dad was in deep shit.

I couldn't cope.

After all of my denials that I wasn't that fragile woman my father expected me to be, I cracked like crystal dropped on concrete.

I didn't write. I didn't run on my treadmill. I didn't even shower.

I did read some books that had been in my to-be-read pile for a very long time.

I also ate well, because I received regular lunches from Dex.

After that first day of Thai soup and tiramisu, I received some variety of tasty store-bought soup and a homemade baked treat every day. Each day, precisely at noon, I received a text informing me of the delivery to the front porch, and on each dessert there was a note attached.

The day after Maddie's visit was rice crispy treats, which would be weird after his initial fancy Italian effort, but they were my favorite childhood snack. Cereal glued together with gooey marshmallow happened to be my ultimate comfort food, and there was absolutely no way that Dex had stumbled onto that nugget by accident. He had to have grilled Mathilde. The puff of sugary sweet air that hit my nose when I opened the Tupperware, pulling pieces off with sticky fingers, and the way the marshmallow melted on my tongue pulled me back to a familiar, warm place. They'd been my nanna's favorite dessert to make, and my favorite to eat as a child.

I didn't immediately open the note. The guy had delivered a food that I usually ate when I was premenstrual or having a very bad day. I expected something...warm. Caring. Sympathetic. Something that would make me cry.

But when I eventually unfolded the sheet of

printer paper, I found exactly one sentence. And I definitely wouldn't call it sympathetic. Mostly just...strange.

If you could be any superhero, who would you be? Dex

It wasn't like I had a pressing schedule and no time to consider the answer. I was basically taking a vacay from life. People who didn't work for themselves called them mental health days. Some people shopped, some hiked, others watched TV. I avoided life by burying myself in books. Some were new from the massive list I called my to-be-read pile, but some were books I'd read before, stories I knew would give me the comfort I needed.

And I also, apparently, answered ridiculous questions posed by incredibly hot men.

Untrue. I'd only answer silly icebreaker questions posed by one nerdy-hot guy.

That was exactly what it was, an icebreaker. A question asked to learn more about the other person without being too intrusive or overly personal. Kind of funny given the fact he knew I was flipping my shit currently. Again, see rice crispy treats.

The man had not just made my favorite comfort food, he'd gone to the trouble to figure out what that was. I was definitely answering his silly question.

It took me a few hours of casual ruminating before I decided on Wonder Woman.

Not particularly inspired, but she was a strong woman in a time when they'd been few and far between, so I was good with it.

I pulled out my cell—which had died. So I charged my phone, ignored the handful of texts that popped up when I turned it back on (Maddie, Mathilde, and a number that looked like spam), and pretended like there wasn't a voicemail from my dad. We chatted pretty regularly, so it wasn't surprising that I'd happened to miss a call from him—but it was bad luck. I wasn't at all ready to talk to him. Not yet.

I typed in my response, then added: *How about you, big guy?*

His reply was swift, like he'd been waiting for me to text. I'm sure that wasn't the case, but it felt like it.

Ant-Man.

Ant-Man was his wannabe superhero?

I waited for an explanation, but none came. I decided to eat more rice crispy treats and check back.

But an hour later he still hadn't explained. Curiosity got the best of me.

· · ·

ME: *Why Ant-Man?*
    Dex: *Why not Ant-Man?*

SERIOUSLY? I might need fortifying before I tackled this. I put the kettle on for tea.

ME: *There has to be a reason that you chose a superhero whose main talent is to shrink to a microscopic size. I thought men were all about bigger being better.*

I HADN'T EVEN CONSIDERED how sexual that might sound. Not even after I hit send.
    I did, however, when he replied.

DEX: *I thought *women* were all about bigger being better. Either way, I'm covered.*

THEN HE ADDED A WINK. Good grief.
    Before I could think of an appropriate response that didn't reference his huge cock, he'd sent another text.

. . .

DEX: *Paul Rudd makes Ant-Man seem like a good choice. Brilliant, funny, strong in a not flashy way, and he can go anywhere.*

ACTUALLY, that was all true. I forgot about the strength thing, but he was right. The Marvel character was witty and smart.

ME: *Ok. You win.*
 Dex: *Definitely, but not because of Ant-Man. Thanks for playing.*

I WAS PRETTY sure that I'd just been complimented. That the "win" was texting with me. Looked like Dex had a little game when it came to women—or he was just that nice of a guy.

Several days and several questions later, I was sold on Dex's sincerity. He was still attaching a daily note with a question, but when I replied, our text conversations weren't limited to his icebreaker.

We'd talk about all sorts of oddball things.

Some serious. I knew he had a brother who'd died when he was quite young. He knew I had a tense relationship with my dad and was currently ducking his calls.

Some less so. I knew he loved arcade games from the eighties, bizarre given he was too young to have experienced them firsthand. He knew I loved huge fluffy sweaters because I felt like I was cuddling inside a blanket when I wore them.

And some personal, like his favorite things. Color, blue; season, summer then winter; weather, and this was an odd one, clear skies.

He made fun of my favorite color, which was velvet, claiming it wasn't a color at all. A point I conceded, but I pointed out that every color was improved when it was expressed through a decent-quality velvet. (Point to me on that one.) He also knew that I agreed with his seasons, though I had winter and fall neck and neck. And my favorite weather was cold and sunny.

There were also little details about our lives that we shared, preferences, habits.

And some not-so-little things. I fessed up to being Kitty Sweet. Via text. A little crazy, since I didn't really tell people about that. I'm sure Maddie could dig it up, but she was a qualified investigator...who claimed to be a monster hunter. Whatever she called herself, she'd found my biological mother in basically a day. She could talk about the fact that Lizbet Jones hadn't been hiding all she wanted, she was a damn good investigator to have managed that.

Like every other time it happened over the last few days, I shoved thoughts of Lizbet and monsters and my dad's unanswered calls right out of my head.

I needed more time.

I needed to process.

I needed to not shatter like a piece of crystal dropped on concrete.

My phone pinged with a text message. Weird. It was too early for lunch—I was still lounging in bed reading—and Mathilde had told me to message if I needed anything. She'd emphasized that she was here for me but didn't want to stress me out with multiple text messages. Which was one of several reasons why we were friends; she totally got me.

The message was from an unknown number. I almost dismissed the notification, but I caught the first few words in the preview. It didn't seem like a spam message, and the number was local.

Unknown number: *You have to come to coffee with me!*

Unknown number: *This is Taylor and I've got a mess and I blame you entirely.*

I STARED AT THE PHONE, waiting for her to explain, because I had no clue what she was talking about.

ME: *Hi?*

    Taylor: *Sorry!*

    Taylor: *No actually. I'm not sorry. I'm mad at you. You made a coffee date with my ex's ex and then didn't go. You were supposed to be my moral support!*

I STARED AT MY PHONE, caught between annoyance and amusement. But all I had to do was remember Taylor and her bouncy personality to know I wasn't really annoyed. Then I did something I very rarely do. I owned up to the crazy behind the curtain. Or at least a little bit of it.

ME: *Personal crisis. Haven't been out much. Apologies for not cancelling ahead of time. How'd it go?*

.   .   .

Poorly, based on her initial text, but it felt polite to ask. I'd actually completely forgotten that I'd made that date. Given everything that happened afterward —meeting Taylor's drunkity-drunk persona, finding out Mathilde was a "witch," Taylor's claim to psychic powers—it wasn't exactly a shock that I'd forgotten to enter the appointment with Susie and Taylor into my calendar. Since it hadn't been on my calendar, I hadn't given it another thought, what with my life imploding and all.

I was a little surprised that Taylor had still thought I'd show, and even more surprised that given that fact she hadn't sent me a reminder text.

Meeting for coffee with your new friend who thought you were whackadoo and the woman you walked in on your fiancé screwing was bound to be awkward. But just meeting with the woman you'd seen reverse cowgirling the man you planned to marry without a buffer at all—that was *extra* awkward.

Mea culpa. I'd not just encouraged that crazy shit, I'd facilitated it.

TAYLOR: *Oh, girl. I didn't go. I was still hungover last Sunday. You know how to do a lush Friday brunch.*

. . .

LUSH. I didn't think that meant what she thought it meant. That or... Were we remembering the same event?

TAYLOR: *I rescheduled. I sort of on purpose forgot to text you to cancel hoping that you'd come this week because Bain said that Dex said that you weren't leaving the house. Then. Not now. Now I don't know, but it's been a while so you should leave your house on Sunday and come with me.*

I READ that text three times. I guess I took too long to parse the mess that pretended to be a sentence, because she texted again.

TAYLOR: *Are you okay? Should I bring booze?*

THERE WAS ONLY one correct answer.

. . .

ME: *No. I'm good. Thanks for asking. No booze. I'm doing fine.*

I ONLY JUST REFRAINED FROM exclamation points and rainbow emojis. Although, I guess I did say that I was doing okay in a few different ways, multiple times. Overkill, my name is Kaylee, aka the woman who was in no state to have Taylor without alcohol anywhere near my home, let alone a booze-wielding Taylor.

TAYLOR: *Awesome! So you can come to coffee with me!*

DAMMIT. I totally stepped into that trap.

I waffled a bit, so Taylor just pushed out the date. Two minutes later, I was committed to a Sunday coffee meeting with Taylor and her ex's hookup—Susie, I really needed to start thinking of her as Susie if I was going to meet her face-to-face—and I had no idea how that had happened. I hadn't showered in days. I didn't even know how many days. I was in no state to be making social obligations for my future self.

I'd been holed up for days.

No direct human contact for days, and I just made a coffee date, which required me to venture out into the world. With *Taylor*.

And I didn't want to spend time with Taylor, because...

Huh.

I kind of *did* want to spend time with her.

She was a whirlwind. And persistent. I liked persistent people. As an introvert and a homebody and a person who spent every day alone but for the company of fictional characters, it took some persistence to befriend me.

Mathilde had been the same way. I hadn't invited her for lunch on an almost daily basis. She'd invited herself. Over and over again.

And now she was my friend. My closest friend in Austin.

So...yeah, I was actually glad that Taylor had basically twisted my arm by acting like the offspring of a southern belle and a bulldozer with more than a hint of ditzy blonde thrown in for fun.

Not that I thought Taylor wasn't bright. I was pretty damn sure that she'd just played me. There was intent behind all that silliness.

Or she'd had a few adult beverages before texting me.

Best not to contemplate that question too deeply.

I hadn't set my phone down for more than a minute when it pinged again. I assumed it was Taylor again.

It wasn't. It was Dex, and he was early.

I'd texted with Taylor while sprawled on my bed. That seemed somehow indecent when the person on the other end of the line was Dex, so I sat up and propped myself against my pillows before opening his message.

Well, that was interesting. He was inviting me to go for a run. Outside, away from my house-cocoon.

It was his first attempt to see me in person since I'd wigged out and left his house in a panic.

He knew from our text conversations that I normally jogged on my treadmill most days. Not this last week, but most days. And I knew that he ran several times a week with his dog, Chelsea. The same dog he wasn't entirely convinced I *wasn't* afraid of.

I wasn't. In retrospect, without the glow, Chelsea looked like she was probably a really nice dog. Gorgeous, but also sweet. I had a vague memory of her worried canine gaze fixating on me as I hyperventilated. Any dog who didn't want me to stop breathing had to be okay, right?

My phone rang.

I picked it up without checking the caller ID. I knew it was him.

"Go running with me."

"Hello," I replied.

"Right. Hi, Kaylee. How are you today?" He paused, but not nearly long enough for me to reply. "Go running with me."

I hadn't left the house in days. Hadn't been on my treadmill. Hadn't done anything but try to forget that the world was out there.

His invitation should have seemed like a bad idea.

"Sure. Give me fifteen." I needed to shower in the worst possible way. No way was I leaving my house like this, even to go run. Actually—especially to go run. I'd stink up the whole neighborhood with my hermit-lady stench. "Dex?"

"Still here."

"Bring Chelsea."

He paused a beat, but then said without much inflection, "Will do."

Kaylee had become a campaign. Similar to a military action, but more delicate. Like with an intelligence op, I prioritized patience over pressure.

Which was basically what I told Bain when he stopped by my house Friday morning.

Bain scowled. "Hit the gym with me. You can do whatever that is later."

"Can't. I'm making crème brûlée." Which was exactly what I'd told him via text when he'd initially asked me half an hour ago.

"At nine o'clock in the morning? Do it later."

"Nope. It's in the oven. I'm not going anywhere." I wasn't about to explain that I'd started it so early because it had to chill for a few hours before I could deliver it to Kaylee's doorstep, where I would then leave it without actually speaking to the woman herself.

Maybe it was time for me to invite her out of the house. Not because I had this awesome strategy worked out. Just because I really wanted to see her.

She sounded better and better each day. Her text replies came faster, and she seemed less in the dumps. But still, I wanted to lay eyes on her. Make sure I wasn't reading the situation wrong and that she was slowly recovering from whatever shock Madeline Van Helsing had delivered. And whatever the hell had happened at my house.

Mathilde told me Kaylee had a follow-up appointment with Madeline and was expecting news about her mother to be delivered. Then she'd had a meltdown. Mathilde's words, and she wasn't the kind to exaggerate. The woman thought the hex hanging over my head was no big deal. If anything, she minimized.

She'd knocked on my door and told me to fix it. That Kaylee had cancelled lunch with her for the foreseeable future. That was definitely a problem. Best I could tell, Mathilde was Kaylee's only friend.

I assumed I was to blame—or whatever had caused Kaylee to have a panic attack at my house was—but Mathilde's intel led to a different conclusion. I had no clue who Kaylee's mother was, but I did know she was a demon.

I also knew that information would be particularly shocking to someone like Kaylee. I'd managed to wheedle some of Kaylee's background out of Mathilde. It seemed Kaylee had exhibited early signs of possessing magic, her father had known about it, and he'd handled the emergence of his child's magic as something like a mental illness.

Which was fucked up. The guy had to know his child was likely to inherit some amount of magic. If Kaylee had been raised by a human mother, then sure, it would be possible to remain ignorant of his child's potential. But a demon doesn't drop a baby with a fully human parent without having "the talk."

Demons were an odd lot. They were insular. They policed themselves. They lived within the human world but apart from it. And they didn't tend to mingle with other magical peoples or humans on a social level. Sex was the exception. They had offspring with humans, though not at any great rate, and otherwise kept to themselves.

I didn't understand them. I did know they didn't love like other creatures, or have the same sort of parental feelings for their offspring that the rest of the world experienced. They were one of the most "other" of the magical peoples.

But they lived by the same precept that the rest of us did: magic was a poorly kept secret, but a secret nonetheless.

A demon wouldn't dump its child with a human parent without making damn sure that provisions were in place for the child's possible possession of magic.

"You want to tell me what's going on? You've been staring at the oven for at least two minutes."

The crème brûlée looked good. Probably needed another three minutes, which was the time left remaining on the timer. Not that I'd been staring at it. I'd been completely checked out and Bain called me on it.

"Just stewing. And contemplating someone's poor parenting skills."

"This has to do with your woman." When I didn't reply, he said, "Fine. Your business, I get it. Any update on your hex?"

My heart rate cranked up immediately.

"No. Just leave it." My denial came out sharper than I intended. But fuck him. I couldn't fix it. I was pretty sure it wasn't permanent—but there wasn't some quick fix spell for my broken ass.

Chelsea trotted into the kitchen. She'd greeted Bain when he first arrived and then disappeared to sulk on her dog bed when he didn't do more than absentmindedly pet her a few times.

She trotted up to me and sat. I'd been edgy in general, which Chels tolerated. She didn't love it, but it didn't stress her out. The near-yelling was another matter entirely.

I knelt next to her and rubbed her chest.

"Man, you're stressing out your dog. What is going on with you? Fix your shit or get over it already."

I looked up at the man I'd known for almost as long as I'd been alive, and I wanted to strangle him.

"Fuck you." The words were casual, but the intent wasn't. "I put up with your ex and the fallout after she was gone. You have no right to give me shit. None."

"I get it. I made bad choices, and you were there for me. But hell, just because I was an idiot doesn't give you an excuse to be a complete dumbass. Learn from the mistakes of others. That's what separates us from the monsters."

Pretty sure he meant animals, but hell, monsters worked, too.

"You don't understand anything." I was bitter,

and I sounded it. The guy had hit gold. Taylor was a weirdo, but she was also a cool person and she was Bain's weirdo. They were perfect for each other, which made sense, because they were mates.

He thought Kaylee was my Taylor. He was wrong. She was amazing, but we weren't mates, whatever Mathilde's faulty love spell had indicated.

He sighed. "I understand more than you think. She's your woman." He stopped and waited for me to look at him. "Your mate. Even if you're not absolutely perfect in this moment, she's still your mate."

"I like her. It's enough for now."

I'd said as much before, with other women. Kaylee seemed different with her shy demeanor and spicy writing. Her fiendish focus when writing, sprinkled with outright ogling of my ass and chest. Her close relationship with the father who'd betrayed her. Her conviction that velvet was a color, when clearly it wasn't. The woman was a writer. She had to understand the basic definition of the word.

Kaylee was different—but she wasn't my mate.

I might not be her perfect prince, but I'd make whatever it was that was happening between us last as long as I could.

Bain was shaking his head. "You pathetic bastard. She's right there. Man up and take her."

Since we hadn't lived in a time of pillaging and kidnapping for a while now, I knew what he really meant was take the opportunity. And I was. I just didn't have the same expectations as my happily mated best friend.

I'd thought briefly, after Bain had found his mate and another dragon out west found his, that there might be hope.

But then I'd been hexed, and my unrealistic hopes had deflated like the balloon of hot air they'd always been. My life wasn't a happily ever after waiting to happen. It never had been. Why would now be any different? Especially now. I'd been fucking hexed. Whatever Mathilde said about the hex being a side effect of making me more suitable as Kaylee's love interest, no way would magic alter me to better suit my true mate.

Since when did soul mates need to be changed to fit together? Clearly Kaylee's Prince Charming would be human if anything Mathilde had told me about the hex was true.

The oven timer went off. I silenced it and pulled out the water-filled pan with the custard dishes. "These are for her, you pushy fucker."

When he didn't reply, I turned to find him grinning. "You haven't given up."

"I like her. Like I said, it's enough for now."

His grin disappeared. "You're going to treat her like some casual fuck. Your future mate. I should kick your ass."

I looked heavenward and thought about cool wind lifting my wings up. When I was fairly certain I wouldn't try to maim my best friend, I said, "Yeah, Bain. I make fucking crème brûlée for all my casual lays." Even saying the words in relation to Kaylee left a foul taste in my mouth. "There's a lot of real estate between a hookup and a mate, buddy. For those of us less blessed by fate, we take what we can get."

"You want to date her." He said it like it was shocking. And wrong.

"She's good enough to be my mate, but not my girlfriend?" I didn't let on that the label felt wrong. He didn't need any encouragement in his lunacy.

"Not what I'm thinking. At all." He examined me, then turned his attention to the perfection of my custard. Then he shrugged. "You know what? I don't have time for your bullshit. I need to get a workout in before I meet my mate for lunch."

It wasn't my imagination that he put some emphasis on the word mate. "You do that." Asshole.

"Yeah. And you give me a call when you've removed your head from your ass. Oh, and say hello to Kaylee from Taylor—although I'm pretty sure they've been texting. Something about meeting up with the witch that was banging her ex-piece-of-shit fiancé."

"He's still alive?" I asked in a pseudo-innocent tone. I knew perfectly well that Taylor had threatened to castrate him if he fucked with her ex.

"Fuck off." And with that pleasantry, he left.

Good thing. If he hadn't, I'd have dragged his sorry ass to the door and shoved him out of my house. I needed to text Kaylee.

KAYLEE

I'd decided to fess up to Dex.

To seeing the glowing dog, having the supposed demon mom, hiring the monster hunter PI. All the things.

I hadn't talked to Mathilde yet, but if this run didn't send me to crazytown, I planned to invite her over for lunch tomorrow and update her, as well.

They'd both been so supportive during my meltdown. I owed them an explanation for my whackadoo behavior over the last several days, even if it caused me stress to discuss it all.

I couldn't hide every time someone mentioned their horoscope, or refuse to mingle with anyone who read tarot. There were things in this world no one could explain. I happened to believe that those currently unexplainable things would eventually be dissected and revealed to have scientific explanations. Not sure how that tied in with glowing dogs, demon mothers, and monster hunter PIs, but there was an explanation beyond everyone I knew was crazy.

But before I could get to the glowing dog or my suspect family tree, I had something else to deal with. Dex. In running tights.

I opened the door to find him kitted out for the cold front that had blown in this morning. Running tights, shorts, and a long-sleeved tech shirt. He looked... Damn. I'd agreed to go running even though I'd known it was cold and damp outside, because I needed to leave my house. And I wanted to see him. But I'd been quietly disappointed that I'd be missing out on ogling the hottest man I'd ever met in running shorts and a tight T-shirt.

I'd been way off base. This worked. This totally worked. Probably because Dex would look hot in anything. The man has the body of a god.

"Hey," he said in an amused tone.

I looked up from his incredible legs encased in skintight running tights, paused to see if I could detect a bulge beneath the shorts he'd layered on top, then finally made my way to his gorgeous smile and his sexy moss-green eyes.

He was definitely laughing at my obvious gawking.

Before I could even think about being embarrassed, I realized we were missing an important component to this run: Chelsea. I'd planned to address my reaction to meeting her before we set out.

"Where's your dog?"

He smiled big enough to flash straight white teeth. "Don't give me your mean look. I deserve better after all those desserts I delivered."

I hadn't realized I was glaring, but it was important he understood I wasn't afraid of his dog. He loved that dog. "And they were all amazing. Thank you so much. Now where's the pooch?"

He stepped to the side, and I saw that Chelsea was sitting patiently on the sidewalk in front of my house.

"Wow. She's really well trained." And she still glowed. Dammit. I was hoping that issue would resolve itself.

But this time I was prepared. I was ignoring it, because it wasn't there.

"I've had her a while," Dex muttered, like he was

hesitant to accept any kind of responsibility for her good behavior. "I thought I'd knock first and double-check you're—"

"Stop. I'm not afraid of your dog."

"Okay?" He looked about as convinced as he sounded.

"Come on." I walked to the absolutely adorable fluffball in front of my house. We never had pets when I was growing up. Dad didn't like the mess.

But I had no idea why I hadn't gotten my own cat or dog. Hell, even a hamster. There was probably some hidden fear there that my therapist—the new one I'd be hiring!—would want to delve into. Really hidden, deep deep down, because I really liked animals.

"Oh my god. She's smiling at me!" Chelsea was wearing a grin that was suspiciously similar to her owner's.

When she heard my excited tone, she glanced at Dex, then stood up and trotted straight toward me. Minus the glow, she was a gorgeous girl. Except there wasn't a glow, because that wasn't real.

I knelt down and petted her. No one liked being loomed over, right? After I'd petted her pretty head, stroked her gorgeous coat, and rubbed her narrow chest, I figured we'd made friends. Her happy expression and wagging tail seemed to support that conclusion as well. I stood up to find an inscrutable expression on Dex's face.

"I told you, I'm not scared of dogs."

"I guess not." His tone was neutral. There was no push for an explanation.

Damn, he was a good guy.

I took a deep breath. He'd already had a peek behind the curtain. I was just going to widen the crack a little. "She glowed."

He glanced at his dog, then me. I couldn't read his expression. But on the bright side, he didn't look like I'd just announced aliens had landed.

I cleared my throat. "Glows, actually. It's all around her. Obviously, she's not really glowing, but to me, she looks like she is. It's a...thing, I have. I guess, a medical condition."

That elicited a frown, then closer study of his dog. He squinted, as if that was going to let him see what I saw. Please.

But then the weirdest thing happened. He smiled. Not just any old smile. Dex's smiles are almost dangerous they're so delicious, but this, this smile stole my breath. And then he laughed. It was deep and rolling. Warm.

He picked up his dog and swung her around like

she weighed nothing. Finally, he said, "You hear that, Chels? You're glowing, sweetheart."

She didn't look in the least offended to be swung around. Then again, when he'd finished, he cuddled her against his chest like a baby, so I guess there was compensation. Her canine nose tipped toward me and she had that same grin she'd worn earlier. Maybe it was just Malinois, with their long, narrow noses and pricked ears. Maybe they all sported that knowing grin. It was just built into their appearance, like basset hounds looked sad and pugs were ugly-cute.

Eventually, Dex set his dog on the ground, and she sighed. I understood where she was coming from. I'd rather be cuddled against Dex's broad chest, too.

And then I was. He hugged me against all those glorious muscles, and then he swung me around, kind of like he had his dog. I should probably be offended, but I couldn't be. His happiness was too contagious.

When he let me go, I kind of wobbled a second before I had my balance. It was disorienting, being snuggled against all that manliness then being set adrift. "Want to tell me what that's all about?"

He grabbed his foot and pulled his heel back against that fine ass of his, stretching his quads. "I thought we were running?"

I rolled my eyes. "Okay, but I have some other weird shit to tell you, and once we start moving, we're not stopping for hugs."

Total lie. I'd stop whatever I was doing—running, breathing air—for more of Dex's hugs. But I doubted that whatever had prompted Dex's weirdly positive response to my first disclosure would be repeated when I started talking demons and monster hunters.

"Do we have a plan?" I asked as we walked briskly down the road.

Chelsea was staying within two feet of Dex without a leash, though I noticed that Dex had one wrapped around his waist. It took a second for us to figure out who would be where. Obviously Chelsea was near the curb, but Dex seemed uncomfortable with me being roadside. I gave him a look and he shrugged, ceding to my superior common sense. Not like someone was going to clip me. We'd be on the sidewalk most of the time.

"Walk five minutes, jog five minutes, run—how long do you usually run on your treadmill?" When I shrugged, he said, "Okay, then we'll run however long you want, then do a five-minute cool out. I'm just here for the awesome company, so whatever is good with me."

The implication being that he could outrun me. To be fair, he probably could. I'd run cross country in high school, but I wasn't more than a casual runner now. Just enough to stretch my legs, get my heart rate up, and keep me from crawling the walls when I wrote. Dex, on the other hand, was not only taller than me, he also looked like working out was his job.

It wasn't. I'd discovered through our text conversations that he managed a few portfolios. It kind of sounded like he was a wealth management guy, the sort of financial advisor who handled just a few clients, but the kind who were fabulously wealthy. Not what I would have guessed, since I'd yet to see him in a suit or anything approaching business attire.

Maybe that was the influence of his military background. He'd been closed-lipped about it, so I suspected he had some difficult memories that he didn't want to share. I totally got that, what with my own experiences that weren't exactly shiny and shareable.

We walked mostly in silence, other than Dex answering vaguely that work was good when I asked. When we started to jog, he called me out. "You mentioned—and I quote—'some other weird shit' that you wanted to tell me."

This might actually work out okay. When you jogged with someone, you were both facing the same direction. Not having to stare into Dex's handsome face as I uttered the boner-killer words "demon spawn" sounded like a great idea to me. "Yeah. So, I hired someone to find my mother."

I wasn't getting into my PI being a monster hunter. I figured I'd get through the demon part of the conversation first.

"Mathilde told me you'd gotten some news on that front. I can't imagine growing up not knowing who one of my parents was. My mother and father were...difficult, but I was fortunate to have them in my life for as long as I did."

He sounded a little bit like he was trying to convince himself of that. Maybe something to do with losing his brother and how that had impacted his family? But today wasn't Pry Into Dex's Past day. It was Peek Behind the Curtain of Kaylee's Crazy day.

"Full disclosure, the PI I hired was Mathilde's

recommendation." I tipped my head slightly so I could catch his reaction without full-on turning and staring.

He nodded, like that was no surprise. "Madeleine Van Helsing. An excellent choice. She's expensive, but she's discreet, thorough, and very good at what she does."

I couldn't argue any of those points, but his comment didn't address the elephant trotting along beside us—and I didn't mean Chelsea. She was light on her feet and not remotely elephant-like, unlike Maddie the Monster Hunter.

"Ah... Do you know what it is that she does? Exactly?"

Dex had these friends who believed in all this strange stuff, but he'd been silent about his own beliefs.

I didn't really know what he thought about love witches and psychics, other than he wasn't judging them in any obvious way and didn't seem to be bothered by what they claimed they could do. He was friendly with Mathilde and Taylor, and he knew everything I knew about them.

"I believe the phrase you're looking for is monster hunter."

"Right." Damn. I didn't think he'd know that.

He didn't explain how he knew about Maddie or what he knew of monster hunters. To be fair, I didn't jump in and ask him.

He just asked, "What did Maddie find out?"

So I went with the flow, and said, "My mom's name is Lizbet Jones."

Did he just flinch? A teeny bit? Hard to say. We'd picked up the pace. It was a little chilly, so as soon as I felt like my muscles were warm, I'd pushed to a faster speed. That meant I wasn't splitting my attention as well between the road and Dex. Old habits. I like to look straight ahead when I run.

"Did she say anything else?" There was something in his tone, a hint that he *knew*.

"Yeah, that my mom is a war demon and would probably be angry as hell that my dad hadn't told her I'd ended up with some magic." I pushed a little faster. It was that, or I'd be checking out Dex's response to my insane statement.

I could already feel my face flushing bright red—and not from the workout or the cold—so I didn't need anything to amplify my current state of acute embarrassment.

We jogged in silence for a few blocks.

Long enough for cool air to chill my cheeks back to a workout level of redness.

Eventually, Dex said, "I've got it, too."

I snorted. "What, a war demon mother?"

It was sweet for him to play along, but really, there was a limit.

"No, magic."

I slowed down and cast a glance his way. He looked serious.

"You believe it all. The love witch stuff, Taylor being psychic, demons."

"Mathilde is a terrible witch, but sure, I believe she's got magic. And Taylor's *a little* psychic. The equivalent of decent intuition, so far as I can tell."

Why did all of that sound so...*normal* coming from Dex?

Except he'd also said that he had magic, too.

"What sort of magic are you supposed to have?" Oh, shit. I hadn't meant to say it like that.

Thankfully, he made an amused sound. Not quite a chuckle, but halfway there. Glad he found my disbelief diverting and not offensive. I really didn't want to hurt his feelings. He was just so *nice*. And fit. He wasn't even slightly out of breath.

"The broken kind."

"You don't sound too thrilled about that. Have

you considered that maybe—" I paused as I considered how to ask a person if they'd considered whether maybe the magic they placed their faith in and failed them might possibly *not be real*?

Not sure there was a great way to ask that.

It didn't matter. He knew where I was going. "It's a recent problem. Trust me when I say I have years of evidence to prove I can do the kind of magic I do."

I glanced at him.

"Do you really want to know?" he asked, once again practically reading my mind.

"I'm not really sure."

"Let me know. I'm happy to tell you. Unfortunately, I can't show you at the moment."

"Because your magic is broken. How does that happen?" It seemed an odd sort of way to describe oneself. I indicated the turn up ahead. It would add a good two miles to our route. We weren't pushing hard—I wasn't; Dex wasn't pushing at all—I'd just warmed up, and I was enjoying stretching my legs and spending time with Dex in a way that didn't seem pressure-filled.

"It's more a question of it being contained. Like someone's wrapped it in cling film."

I wanted to hug him. I wouldn't like any part of me being wrapped in plastic. A big warm blanket was cozy. Cling film was claustrophobic—and sweaty. Since I was a writer and all, I decided to use my words. Whether I believed in his magical powers or not, he clearly did. "I'm really sorry that happened to you."

He tipped his chin down and toward me. I could see the smirky smile he was halfheartedly trying to repress. "Thanks." Then the smile faded and he added, "I'll get it fixed. Somehow."

I got the impression this magic business was a big deal to him. Which was just bizarre. He was this handsome, successful, charming guy with a nice home and a job he seemed to like, all sorts of time to pursue his interest at the library or the gym, and good, long-term friends.

And yet, he believed in magic.

Maybe the friends were the issue. Maybe he'd been sucked into the fantasy.

"At some point, you're going to realize that it's not all in your head." I started to protest, but he said, "Hang on. Let me just say this."

I huffed out an annoyed breath. "Sure. But only because you made me carrot cake yesterday with the best cream cheese icing I've ever had in my life."

The smirk was back. "I've got crème brûlée in the fridge for later."

This guy. I hadn't a clue why he'd decided he needed to feed me, but I wasn't about to protest. I'd already done that after the third day. He'd ignored me and continued to deliver soup and tasty home-made treats. I wasn't an idiot. I wasn't going to pitch a hissy fit over his kindness. And the food. Oh my God, so good.

"Crème brûlée sounds amazing," I admitted. "Go ahead. Hit me with your cult sales pitch."

This time there was no mistaking his flinch, because he stuttered a step. I double-checked that I hadn't gone too far, but he was just shaking his head. "There is such a big 'I told you so' happening in your future."

I waited for the selling to start. How much magic could do for me. How it would change my life. How, once I'd discovered it, I would never go back. Belief systems, diets, politics, they all had their spiel that was geared to win over the naysayers.

Or maybe he'd go the route Maddie had taken. Just lay out some "facts." Like the alternate reality they believed was *the* reality. Not quite gaslighting, but only by a thin thread. I didn't for a moment believe that Maddie had been trying to pull the wool over my eyes. I believed that she believed.

"Magic is real. It's all around us, and you can see it. It's genetic in your case. Usually, it's genetic."

Exactly what I'd believed as a child. That the fantasy tales I read were real. The glowing was magic. The wings belonged to fairies. That Harry was truly alive and my pet.

Actually, Harry might be the reason I'd never had a pet. I'd cried and cried when Dad told me I couldn't play with Harry. And then Harry had vanished. Gone, as if he'd never been. I remember accusing Dad of taking him away.

Damn. Not what I wanted to be thinking about while I was running next to a guy who smelled like baked goods and looked like the god of perfect lumberjack sporty men.

Focus, lady.

Also, where was the rest of his join-my-freaky-magic-cult spiel?

"That's it? That's your sales pitch?"

"No pitch. I'm not trying to sell you on it. It simply is." He pointed to a street that would eventually take us back to our neighborhood. We'd ventured into an area adjacent to ours.

"Yeah, probably a good idea. I think I'm going to be well over my usual distance today."

"You're in good shape, and we won't top six miles.

You should be fine." He managed to say all that in a much less skeevy way than I would have. I'd have made some comment about his ridiculously low body fat, his cut abs, or his bubble butt, if I'd commented on his fitness level.

Not commenting on his bitable ass. "Probably still a good idea to cool out properly and stretch, but I'm sure you're right. I'll be fine. Nothing else to say on the genetic mutation front?"

"Not a mutation. You just happen to have one parent who isn't human. You should talk to your dad."

I frowned. "Maddie said that, too. If y'all knew my dad, you really wouldn't be saying that. He's going to lose his mind when I tell him I hired an investigator to find my mother. I've actually ducked his calls the last few days."

Maybe more than a few days. A few implied two to three. It might be more like a week now.

"Okay, I'm feeling it in my legs now. Entertain me with fun stories of young Dex."

"Ah. Those aren't so entertaining. Lots of training, not much fun."

"Oh, I knew it! Taylor mentioned that you and Bain and Archer were friends from way back and I guessed that you'd been on a sports team together in college. It was college, right? Football? Or hockey?" I'd have checked out his ass again, but I knew if I slowed he'd keep pace with me.

He was an ideal running partner. Fit enough to go do whatever I wanted and talk through the entire run, completely without ego or concern for his own run, and smelled amaaaazing.

I inhaled deeply. How did he smell like cake when we were running?

"I never played college ball, though I have played some soccer and I've skated a little. And no, Bain and Archer didn't go to college with me. We know each other from when we were younger."

"Oh, I bet you guys were trouble. Pranking the neighbors, smoking in the parking lot at school." I'd guess Dex smoked some weed, but not Bain. He didn't seem the type to enjoy letting go.

"Not exactly."

"Don't tell me you weren't troublemakers."

He laughed. "Yeah, okay. We were that."

Then he told me a story that involved borrowing his neighbors' horses, another where the three of them had to wrangle some wild goats, and then there was something that involved borrowing another friend's plane. Minus their proclivity for theft, it all seemed pretty harmless.

"So let me get this right: you can ride a horse bareback, know how to milk a goat, and can fly a plane."

"Yes."

"You, Dexter Brodie, are a man of many talents."

"And that's just the boring stuff."

Boring my ass. He'd managed to keep me entertained with his stories all the way home, and I hadn't been kidding about my legs. They were pleasantly noodle-like now that we'd hit the tail end of our run. If I wasn't careful, I was going to have some real soreness day after tomorrow.

We slowed to a walk as we turned down my street, and I had this sudden urge to be honest. The kind of honest that made me feel like a vulnerable dweeb—or a recently picked scab.

"I really appreciate you inviting me out today. I needed to get out of my house. Out of my head. Move a little." I grinned at him. "Or a lot. I'm going to sleep so well tonight."

He wasn't looking at me. His gaze was fixed on something ahead of us. I followed his gaze to a car parked in front of my house.

My dad's car.

"Shit."

He put his hand on my arm, stopping me.

Chelsea immediately came to heel and sat. "You recognize the car?"

There was tension in his voice that I didn't entirely understand.

"Oh, yeah. That's my dad's."

He relaxed visibly.

"Sorry. I didn't mean to worry you." Not that I understood exactly why he was worried. "Like I said before, I've been ditching his calls. But I never imagined he'd drive to Austin. What the hell, right?"

And in about sixty to ninety seconds, he was going to spot me.

"Do you think he might be concerned for you?" Dex maintained a neutral expression and tone, but I could tell he'd picked a side and it was my dad's.

"Please. He can be concerned in Houston."

"He was, until you stopped answering your phone."

I groaned. Now I felt terrible. But Dex didn't get it. He didn't understand my relationship with my father.

"Are you introducing me?"

I blinked, surprised. I hadn't thought one way or the other, but Dex had to walk right by my house to get to his. "You'd meet my dad?"

"Hell, yes."

More surprising than his willingness to "meet the parent" was how eager he seemed at the opportunity.

"Yeah, that's not happening. Not when you're all, your poor dad. He must be so worried."

Dex chuckled. "Not what I said."

"Totally what you meant." But then on impulse, I hugged him. "Thank you, though. For everything."

He held me against his chest, told me, "Anytime," and I'd swear he sniffed my hair.

But I didn't have time to really think about whether that was weird or hot, because my dad was waiting for me on my porch.

Suddenly, I felt like a guilty sixteen-year-old, sneaking into the house with the smell of beer on my breath.

I hated being at a disadvantage with him.

"Call me later. If you need to talk."

I pulled my gaze away from my dad, who I'd spotted sitting on one of my porch chairs, texting. Dex's concerned gaze gave me a little boost of courage, and I nodded.

Then I was off to confront my past and a handful of my childhood insecurities.

I had a name for my mother, a wild story about

my birth, and a newfound confidence regarding the shit that I wasn't supposed to be seeing.

So what if it wasn't there? I wasn't crazy.

And I wasn't fragile.

And I could fucking do this.

When she'd squealed with pleasure over Chelsea, it felt like my heart was growing inside my chest. My two favorite girls, getting along. Pretty fucking awesome.

When she'd asked about my childhood exploits, I'd felt shame, then nostalgia. I'm not sure I'd ever be able to remember my childhood without feeling guilt that I'd lived, when my brother—my parents' perfect, beloved son—had not, but this was the first time I'd looked back on that time and been able to pluck a golden memory from amidst the sewage. The goat story was just before my brother died.

Even the moments of silence had been warm and comfortable. Kaylee was an excellent running partner. Her form was solid, her stamina and fitness greater than she'd implied, but yet she wasn't so focused on meeting her training goals that we couldn't alter our path and our pace, nor was she so focused we couldn't just talk. I wanted to run with her every day. Forget that treadmill bullshit. If I had my way I'd get her out on the streets with me.

And when I saw that car in her driveway, I wanted to dent someone's skull. First, because I thought it was her lover's. I'd never asked her if she was seeing anyone and assumed from our interactions that she wasn't. But then, I'd seen her fear, and I'd wanted to do more than crack a skull. I'd wanted to eviscerate whomever had dared to frighten her.

But it wasn't a lover parked in her drive. It was her father's car, because she hadn't been returning his calls. Not even with a text message to let him know she was safe.

And she was confused by his appearance why? Foolish woman. She didn't understand her worth. Of course he drove a few measly hours to check on her. I had good reason to dislike the man, but at least it seemed he truly cared for his daughter.

In less than an hour, I'd experienced guilt and jealousy, pleasure, warmth, comfort, and affection. I'd experienced all of that—all of those *emotions*—in the span of a short run.

Basically, Kaylee made me feel all the feels, as Taylor would say.

It was an uncomfortable thought. I'd never been like this with a woman before. So open, so honest. So vulnerable.

Not that she was my mate.

History proved that mating wasn't simply a question of connecting with a woman. Archer had so fallen for a woman that he'd lost his way for a few centuries, and he'd never had any illusions that she'd been his mate.

And knowing wasn't always all that easy. Bain had falsely believed himself to be mated. His feelings hadn't been a true indication that he'd found his mate.

Which left me with nothing more than a gut feeling, and my gut said no. My perfect person, the mate of my soul, wouldn't arrive in one of the moments when I was least like myself, not even capable of shifting, barely capable of defending myself, let alone another.

As I rounded the corner, just two houses from my home, I spat out, "Son of a bitch."

Chelsea looked at me like I was a traitor.

Kaylee wasn't the only one with an unexpected visitor. Archer, the bastard, was waiting in my house.

I assumed. His car was in my driveway, and he was nowhere to be seen. He'd have no difficulty breaking into my house.

Chelsea had either caught his scent or recognized his car, because her tail was wagging excitedly. She worshipped him. He knew all the best places to scratch and usually brought a toy when he came over. Not that I'd seen much of him recently.

I let myself in the side door and tested the air for his scent. Ever since Bain met Taylor, he'd barely been around. I liked to think he wouldn't begrudge our friend the love and affection of a mate, but I was starting to have concerns.

"In the kitchen," he called. He was probably helping himself to my provisions.

Chelsea scrambled on the slick floor in her haste to find him.

I stripped off my shirt as I walked through the laundry room, pausing long enough to throw it in the washer. Unlike Archer and Bain, I did my own damn laundry, and I didn't like my workout gear to sit in my laundry basket with my regular clothes.

By the time I got to the kitchen, Chelsea was ensconced in Archer's lap with a stuffed bunny clenched in her teeth. He wasn't eating my food, just bribing my dog.

He set her on the ground, and she trotted off to destuff the bunny. I'd be picking up fluff all over the house for the next two days.

"I hear you're dating a war demon's daughter." He was brushing Chelsea's hair off his chest, so he wasn't looking at me when he added, "I hope she's good in the sack, because that is some serious rage you're playing with."

One, fuck him. That was what he said to me after being practically AWOL for months.

Two, this was *Kaylee* he was talking about.

"Do we need to take this conversation outside?" My tone was neutral and my posture relaxed, but Archer wasn't an idiot. And neither was I; I wasn't about to beat the shit out of him inside my house, where my shit could get broken.

He looked up, saw the look on my face, and said, "Fuck." He ran a hand through his too-long hair. "Hell, I'm sorry, Dex. I'm sure she's a nice girl. I mean, I'm sure she's a great lady. My head's just been up my ass recently."

He wasn't looking great. Shadows under his eyes, scruff that exceeded the fashionable few days' worth he normally sported. His typically well-groomed self was absent today.

In fact, he looked like shit.

"What the hell is going on with you?" I looked closer. "Is that grease under your nails?"

He looked down, then clasped his hands together. "Yeah. Been working on a car."

Something was going on with him. All of us were flush. That happened when you lived beyond human life spans in a world set up for lives that lasted seventy to ninety years. But Archer was ridiculously wealthy. Bain distilled amazing whisky, I managed other people's money (mostly my friends'), and Archer turned two thousand dollars into ten, then did it again and again and again.

He also liked to live like a guy who had a billion or two stashed away. Not ostentatiously, but he paid people to take care of the miscellaneous inconveniences of life, like shopping, cleaning, and home maintenance. Like car maintenance.

The pretentious ass had a majordomo and a housekeeper. He did not fix cars.

"Don't give me that look, asshole. I'm handy."

He was. Hard not to be when you'd lived as long as we had. But... "You've picked up a new hobby, and it's working on cars."

"No, fuckhead. I said I was working on *a* car." He shook his head. "Doesn't matter. It's a long story. Tell me about... What's her name?"

He definitely knew her name. Bain had to have told him about her or he wouldn't be here. He was fucking with me.

"Kaylee."

He flashed a shit-eating grin, like I'd proved some point he was trying to make. "Tell me about Kaylee."

I scowled. "Don't say her name like that. Have a little respect."

His expression morphed. Softened. He looked almost sincere, if that were possible for Archer. "You think she's the one?"

"Not like you mean, not my mate. But she's special."

He stared at me a little too hard for a little too long.

"What?" I prompted. "Just say it."

"You need to leave the past in the past."

I stared, incredulous. Of all people, the man who clung to an ancient heartbreak was telling me I needed to move on.

His jaw clenched and his nostrils flared. Then he caught a glimpse of his hands, stained with grease. "I'm trying. Can you say the same?"

At least I knew why he had grease under his nails. That car he was fixing somehow had to do with a woman.

"I'm interested in a woman, and I'm spending time with her. Isn't that enough?"

Archer looked at me, then his eyes glinted with some strong emotion. "Holy shit. You haven't slept with her, have you?"

I turned my back on him, moving to the kitchen to retrieve a glass of water.

Not that I minded admitting I hadn't slept with her, even though he'd take it entirely the wrong way. It was more that I didn't want to talk to Archer, man-whore, playboy, fucker of more women than I cared to count, about Kaylee. She was sweet. She was nice. Okay, she was sexy and hot as fuck. But mostly, she was just Kaylee, and sex, Kaylee, and Archer did not belong in one conversation together.

By the time I returned to the table with a glass of water for me and a beer for Archer, he was looking contrite. "None of my business."

"Exactly right," I agreed amiably.

"But I do want to say one more thing before I drink this beer and the other seven in your fridge."

I sighed, but I also drank my water and kept my mouth shut. This was bound to be good.

"You're perfect just as you are."

I almost choked on my water, because he looked

completely serious. To hell with being silent. "What the fuck are you talking about? Don't tell me. You've found Jesus."

"What?" He pushed back in his chair, taking his beer with him. "No. Fuck you. I'm trying to be real here, and you're giving me shit." He took a drink, then opened his mouth and spouted some more insanity. "Your parents were asshats, your brother wasn't any more perfect than any other moderately well-behaved fifteen-year-old who's good at kissing ass, and it wasn't your fault he died. There. I said it." He chugged half his beer.

Not where I would have guessed this conversation was headed.

"You broke into my house to give me a bunch of affirmations and to talk about shit that went down literally hundreds of years ago."

He sat there, looking like he was actually considering my words. Then he tipped his beer in my direction. "Yes, except for the breaking in part. Is it really breaking in when you make it that easy?"

I scrubbed my hands over my face.

"Archer..."

"Yo." He stood up, no doubt to get himself another beer.

I shook my head. I had no clue where this was coming from.

Actually, yes, I did. Probably sparked by a combination of shit going down in his life that he wasn't sharing and Bain gossiping about me and Kaylee.

When he returned with a beer for each of us, I said, "I haven't blamed myself for my brother's death in a long time."

He nodded. "Right."

"And I didn't think he was perfect. No one's perfect." But he'd been damn close. He was such a good kid. Not at all an ass-kisser, like Archer had said, just not a complete delinquent like me and my friends.

"Right." That sounded as convincing the second time as the first.

"Whatever. Cheers." I lifted my beer. "To your new hobby. I hope she's worth the trouble."

His eyes narrowed, but he still drank.

Archer didn't stay for seven beers, just the two. Before he left, I asked if he wanted to tell me anything.

He'd been acting oddly for a while now. Not around much, skipping out on some of our guys' nights, and now showing up with grease under his nails.

But he avoided any further mention of what was going on in his life. Instead, he told me that I needed to let go.

Bizarre advice coming from him. Also, I was generally the most mellow of the three of us. The least likely to hold onto old grudges—or old hurts.

He seemed to think I was wallowing in a past that was so far distant I barely thought about it at all. Pot, kettle. Because if ever there was a guy who couldn't escape his own history—more specifically his broken heart—it was Archer.

One woman, all those years ago, and he just couldn't get over it. Not the woman. Any love he'd felt for her had died a very long time ago. No, it was the memory of the pain he couldn't leave behind.

Maybe he was trying. Maybe he wasn't really. Time would tell.

"I need to take a shower." I looked at his beer.

"I'll head out after I finish this. I need a few minutes of quality Chelsea time." Then he walked out of my kitchen, beer in hand, ditching me to play with my dog.

Something was definitely going on with him.

20

KAYLEE

My life is a lie.

My childhood was a lie. In the span of thirty minutes, my father just blew up my entire childhood.

Magic was real.

My mother was a war demon.

And I showed signs of seeing magic and having magic since I was a small child.

My dad, who loved me dearly, had been terrified that he would lose me. Just as Maddie had explained, there'd been an agreement. My father would raise me without interference from my mother—unless I inherited magic. Then she would take me and train me to control and use my magic.

Based on this agreement, I should have been

relinquished to a stranger. A woman I'd never met and who hadn't bothered to know me even though she'd given birth to me.

I had mixed feelings about this obviously. On the one hand, I knew my father loved me, wanted to protect me, and couldn't bear the thought of giving me up. On the other, how could he not be aware of the damage he'd done by lying to me for *years*? And not just during my childhood when I would have had difficulty keeping such a secret. Well beyond.

I was thirty-one years old. I was a fucking adult, with a job and a life apart from my dad's. Why had he continued to lie to me?

I asked him, and he had no good answer. Something about being afraid. But of what? Losing me? Messing up my life? He didn't say. But then, I was hardly in a state of mind to listen with an open heart or mind. I was angry.

He asked if he could stay. I said no, but I promised to call, because in the end, I loved my father. We even hugged.

This was a pivotal moment in our relationship. There was a not-so-subtle shifting of power. I was no longer the fragile child to be protected. I was the grown woman beginning a journey. And not just any journey. Not a new job or marriage or children. I was venturing down a path unfamiliar to him to a place he couldn't follow.

Actually, it had to suck being the father of a kid who could see and do things he could only imagine. I hugged him again and told him I loved him. But then I sent him home.

Then I showered, because I'd just run several miles and I could feel my muscles starting to protest. Also, I smelled.

But then, after I'd gotten out of the shower, put on a pair of jeans and my snuggliest sweater, there was only one place I wanted to be.

Three minutes later I was standing in front of Dex's house about to knock when a tall, lean, dark-headed man opened the door. Not so broad or muscular as Dex, but still a big guy.

I stepped back surprised, but then I realized who he had to be. "You're the third one. Archer."

He didn't look surprised by my unconventional greeting, and since he grinned, I must have guessed correctly.

"Kaylee, right?"

I blushed, because if he knew my name, then Dex was telling his friends about me.

"Get lost, asshole." Dex's grumbly command

came from somewhere over Archer's shoulder. Someone sounded awful cranky.

Archer didn't look remotely put out by his friend's rudeness. He simply slipped past me as he wished us both a good day. He went straight to the car in the drive, the one I hadn't even noticed.

I put that down to my single-minded focus. I was all about Dex. And sex.

Who knew I got horny when my life blew up?

Not me, but then I'd never before discovered that my "overactive imagination" wasn't fantasy. That it was all absolutely real.

I'd been skating on the edge of belief for days now. But today was the day I fell over the edge and into the land of magic. Witches, psychics, and war demons inclusive.

Which begged the question: what exactly was the nerdy-hot lumberjack in front of me?

Dex stood in the doorway, hair wet, like he'd just gotten out of the shower. His visitor must have delayed his post-run shower just like mine had.

"We're having sex."

"Okay." He cocked his head. "Not sure what you were expecting, but I'm not about to say no. We have insane chemistry. I've been attracted to you since I first saw you stalking me at the library."

"There was no stalking. I didn't even know what kind of car you drove until you showed up at that brunch place and offered me a lift home."

It was a weak argument considering how much time I spent watching him.

And exactly how creeped out would he be to find that I'd based a character on him?

Shit.

He reached out a hand and smoothed away the wrinkles in my forehead. "Whatever you say, but I liked it."

"Oh." He liked being "stalked" by me? I was pretty sure he was kidding and just liked that I showed interest in him, but just in case... "To be clear, I didn't even scope out your reading material. I absolutely respected your privacy."

"Thank you. Glad you settled that." Then he kissed me.

Except it wasn't just a kiss. There were tongues and lips involved, but there was also an exchange of air. Like we were breathing for one another.

And then all the warmth was gone. The pressure of his mouth on mine, the feel of his hard chest and abs pressed against me vanished.

It took a second for me to open my eyes.

Mossy-green eyes looked down at me. "You want to ask me something?"

Oh, right. I'd meant to do that. Before the lips and the chest and all the hotness that was Dex touching me.

"Ah, right. Yes. I..." I blew out a breath, inhaled, and tried again. "What exactly are you?"

I couldn't help a bit of a wince. Which was silly. I didn't sense anything bad in Dex. The opposite was true. And the man *baked* for me.

"Dragon."

I blinked, because—"What?"

Even as a kid I hadn't seen anything that remotely resembled a dragon.

He rubbed his jaw, which meant he rubbed his beard. And now *I* wanted to rub his beard. Dragon, dinosaur, whatever. Didn't care.

But then I realized my lust was blinding me to some overt clues. The jaw rubbing, for one. Also, the sexy, mischievous glint in his eyes was fading a bit. I couldn't help a surreptitious glance downward. Um, yeah. He might be slightly conflicted, but his dick was one hundred percent on board.

But I wasn't just about his dick. I was about Dex.

I stretched up on my toes and kissed the corner of his mouth. I also groped his beard. Groped, stroked—same difference. I couldn't pass on the opportunity. But then I said, "I don't know exactly what that means that you're a dragon, but I'm sure it's fine."

I was talking out of my ass here. I had no idea if it was fine. Maybe dragons only had sex with other dragons? Maybe dragons were celibate until marriage.

Hmm. Probably not that last one. Dex didn't strike me as a celibate sort of person. But I wasn't thinking about that, because that meant he'd had sex with other women, and that made me want to choke the life from those women. I wasn't usually violent. It was a disturbing turn for my thoughts to take. Definitely best avoided.

On the bright side, I'd just reassured Dex that *he* wasn't a problem, whatever he was. It was so freeing not being the problematic person in a relationship. Not worrying about hiding my "problem."

"I can't shift."

I shook my head, still not really sure what he was telling me.

"I can't take my dragon form. It's bound." His eyes warmed, and my lady parts did the same. "It's complicated, but that's why I was so glad you could see a glow around Chelsea."

He had been awfully happy about the news.

I stepped inside the doorway.

He stepped back. "You see magic that I can't see."

I nodded, like I was listening. But, real talk, I was only thinking about one thing.

Suddenly, Dex grinned. He picked me up, backed up further inside the house, and shut the door in one fluid motion.

Then his lips were on mine. Again. Finally.

I wrapped my legs around him tighter and he squeezed my ass while he supported my weight. So talented, my dragon.

Oh. My. God.

Dragon.

Drake.

My book.

I leaned back, just enough to see the expression on his face. "I've been writing a romance about a dragon. His name is Drake, and he's inspired by you."

We were moving through his house, but I didn't look at the passing scenery. I just kept my eyes on his.

"That's convenient."

"Not really," I grumbled.

Then the sexiest thing ever happened. He

laughed. That deep, rolling laugh of his, and pressed close like I was to him, I could feel the vibration of it at my very core.

I about swooned.

And maybe ground up on him like a horny wench.

And kissed his neck.

In between gasping, "Yes, yes, yes."

Damn, but Dex was a sexy bastard. I wanted to nibble his neck, and grind against him, and tear his shirt off all at the same time.

So I did.

He helped with the shirt. And all of my clothes. And the rest of his clothes.

"Holy shit." I was leaning back on his bed, completely naked, looking at his fine body—and his enormous erection.

He looked down like he was surprised. Which was funny, because that was his dick after all. I'd have thought he was used to its gargantuan proportions since he lived with it.

"Not sure that's gonna fit."

He laughed that amazing laugh of his. This time it was a chuckle that sent tingles through my body. And since I was apparently programmed to get wet when Dex sexy-laughed, I squirmed on the bed. And then my legs, all on their own, fell open.

Here I was, like an unwrapped present, waiting on his bed for him.

I'd swear I saw a glint in his eyes. Literally, like a glow. Knowing it wasn't my imagination, that I could see actual, real magic, and that Dex was so hot for me his eyes had sparked, really did it for me.

I must have looked as turned on as I was, because Dex groaned, except it sounded almost like a growl, and he fell on top of me—but only after he gave that massive cock of his a good tug.

His mouth was on mine, kissing me, devouring me.

Something niggled in the back of my mind as the firm length of his cock pressed against my thigh. And then it hit me. "Condom," I gasped.

He kept kissing me, just moved to my jaw and my neck.

I needed to remember...something. But I was falling under the spell of his lips and his tongue and his—oh my God. He licked my pulse point, and I lost my train of thought.

What had I been thinking? The thick, heavy length of him nudged closer to home, near the crease of my thigh. "Condom! Please tell me you have a condom!" My voice was squeaky and frantic.

"I'm clean, and I can't get you pregnant." His amused tone wasn't amusing. My brain didn't want to brain...think...make decisions. Whatever. Then he said, "Do you want me to get a condom?"

I wanted him bare inside me. I wanted him as close as he could be with no barrier between us.

That was horny me talking.

But...I trusted Dex. I wasn't on birth control, but also—he was a dragon. Maybe we weren't compatible?

He started to get up, and I made a snap decision.

I grabbed his shoulder. "You can't get me pregnant."

"Not right now." Weird answer, but I believed him. I trusted him. He'd never lied. Waited a while to drop the dragon truth bomb, but never lied and told me as soon as was reasonable.

"You're clean."

Without hesitation, he said, "Yes."

I nibbled my lip and ran my hands over his muscular shoulders to the curve of his biceps. "I'm clean."

He kissed my neck, then whispered in my ear. "Your call. I can get a condom...or not."

This decision shouldn't have been left to horny me. Horny me had bad judgment. Or did she? Because it all came down to trust.

"No condom." And I said it with confidence.

Which apparently pushed Dex's buttons, because he growled. There was no mistaking that sound for a groan. It was a sexy-as-fuck growl. It was like his laugh amplified by a hundred. The sound traveled through my body like a wave of "fuck me now" and landed right at my core.

I bucked against him, and he growled again, this time against my neck.

It crossed my mind that I might get bossy with him if he didn't get a move on—but then I wasn't thinking anything.

Just feeling.

His mouth on my breast, suckling my nipple, then the other.

His hand running along my ribs, the curve of my waist, grasping my ass.

Oh. My. God.

His fingers grazed my clit, then lower. He dipped inside me, then used my own desire to lubricate his fingers as he worked my clit. He thrust two fingers inside me and I had to smother a laugh, because as big as his hands were, those fingers weren't anything on that huge cock of his. He was never going to fit.

And that was when he started to talk.

I was beautiful, amazing, gorgeous. Something to do with chocolate and honey. Something about how hot it was that I was so ready for him. Something about my tits. Luscious. I had luscious tits. I whimpered.

His fingers worked me, first two and then three. Still nothing compared to his cock. He must have felt me tense, because he started making soothing noises as he kissed my belly, then lower.

My hips shot off the bed when he suckled my clit, because I was coming. And coming. His fingers thrust inside me and it wasn't enough. My hands were in his hair and I pressed him closer until I collapsed.

I had never felt so satisfied and so needy at the same time. As my heart thudded in my chest and I tried to catch my breath, I thought about opening my eyes and demanding he give me his cock—but I couldn't. I was a noodle.

A needy noodle.

"Babe, what is a needy noodle?"

I flung my hand over my eyes. "I didn't say that."

He chuckled, then kissed the inside of my thigh.

Unfair. The muscle quivered as his beard made love to my leg. But I couldn't move. I was wrecked, and I hadn't even gotten the full Dex experience. I was kind of pissed, but it didn't seem fair to complain, having just experienced the second-best orgasm of my life.

And yes, I knew it was weird that the best orgasm of my life had been with Dex...in a dream.

Not to say that real-life Dex in any way failed to measure up to dream Dex. The opposite. Real-life Dex told me my tits were luscious. Which was really nice, because I always sort of thought my breasts were on the average side. I liked them, I just—

And then my brain stopped because he kissed my hip.

And my stomach.

My belly button. The soft skin right above the narrow strip of hair I hadn't completely waxed away. The crease of my leg.

Oh my God, he just licked me. Bottom to top, like an ice cream cone, twirling the cherry on top.

Was that moan me?

Fuck yes it was.

His fingers tightened on my hips, because I was squirming and bucking against his mouth. I yanked his hair hard, and finally gave in and he lifted his head.

I glared at him, because he needed to know I meant business. "I want you."

His smile was crooked and gorgeous. "You've got me."

I was soaked, thank fuck, because his giant cock was there, pushing at my entrance. This wasn't going to work. Even dripping wet and desperately turned on, he wasn't going to fit.

Then he started to talk about my luscious tits again and the finest ass he'd ever seen, and he was inside me. He was so big, but also careful and slow. Committed to making this good. I relaxed, and the tightness I felt eased.

He inched in further and I realized that I was holding my breath, but only because he whispered softly in my ear, "Breathe."

As I exhaled, he thrust deeper. I felt so incredibly full. It was amazing. And terrifying.

There was nothing between us. No condom. No secrets, no lies.

I opened my eyes and found his mossy-green gaze watching me. Gauging my feelings, making sure I was still good. I loved that he did that. It was so Dex to take care of me, even now. I loved that about him.

Oh, fuck.

I loved *him*.

I gasped as he thrust the final few inches. My eyes burned, and I was pretty sure I was going to cry. I had never felt so close to another person in my life.

He started to move, still watching me. Not that it was hard to read me, since I was yelling, "Yes!" and "More!" like a fucking porn star.

And when I came, it was so much better than my dream. Because in real life, Dex followed me over the edge and I got to watch the expression of complete surrender on his face. He was so incredibly fucking gorgeous.

21

DEX

Kaylee was my mate.

I wasn't nearly so shocked as I might have been if Bain and Archer hadn't both pointed it out.

It hadn't been obvious. Not to me. Not until now.

The urge to bite her, mark her, had been incredibly intense. Never have I had even the smallest urge to mark a woman as my mate, but with Kaylee it was almost overpowering.

I'd never do it without her consent, but fuck, I'd wanted to.

A cute snuffle emerged from under the chocolate-honey strands of Kaylee's hair. She was sprawled next to and half on top of me, her hair covering her face entirely.

That snuffle turned into a snort, and then she started to snore.

Not quietly.

I did my best not to laugh, because I didn't want to wake her.

Either I wasn't quiet enough or my abbreviated mirth jostled her, because the snoring stopped and she rolled over on her side. Damn, my woman had a fine ass.

She started to snore, but much more quietly this time. More akin to heavy breathing than sawing logs.

I ran my hand down her back, testing the waters. We probably should talk. There was still so much I needed to ask her and tell her. But the smooth skin of her back and her tousled hair were too tempting.

She moaned prettily, like she was thinking dirty thoughts in her sleep.

I cupped her ass, my fingers just grazing her wet slit. Oh yeah, she was definitely having dirty thoughts in her sleep.

All the blood in my body rushed to my cock.

I'd been half-hard before—how could I not be with a gorgeously naked Kaylee right next to me?— but now my balls ached.

I molded my hands over her ass, and she

moaned again, this time with the addition of a sexy little whimper, like she was pissed I hadn't petted her sweet pussy like I had before. She was so fucking sexy.

She wasn't one of those women who had deep curves. She was too fit, too sleek. That was the perfect description for her figure; she was all sleek curves. Her ass was perfectly heart shaped and her tits were fucking luscious. High and round with pretty dark-rose nipples that flushed like berries when I sucked them.

I reached over her shoulder and flicked her hair out of the way. A pebbled nipple waited for me.

My mouth watered, but I didn't want to wake her, so I petted and lightly pinched instead of leaning over and kissing it. When her hips started to move, I leaned close and bit her earlobe. She moaned my name. Fuck, I loved hearing her say my name. She made me feel like a fucking god, the way she'd chanted it over and over again when she was coming.

"Are you too sore?" I asked as I petted her wet slit.

That was me being a gentleman. What I wanted to say was: is it okay if I fuck you from behind, or are you too raw from the thorough dicking I already gave you?

I had manners.

"Oh. My. God." She panted and pushed back against my hand. "Not too sore. Not too sore."

I took that as permission to nudge my cockhead against her wetness. When she made sweet mewling noises, I played a bit, rubbing the head up and down, making sure she was nice and wet, ready for a second round. She was dripping. She'd definitely been having dirty dreams. Fine by me, as long as I was starring in them.

Holding her tit in one hand, I rolled the peak as I entered her from behind. Unlike last time, I didn't have to slowly stretch her as I entered her. It was a snug fit, but I wasn't worried I might hurt her.

Once I was fully seated, I moved my hand from her pretty pink nipple to her clit.

I played with the swollen nub as I slowly fucked her.

She was very appreciative.

And when she came just seconds before me, it was with my name on her lips. *Dex, Dex, Dex…*

22

KAYLEE

Late-afternoon light shone through Dex's window, bringing out the red in his beard. He had freckles on his shoulders. Faint but visible now with the light shining on his still form. I'd not seen that before.

I hadn't had a chance to really look at Dex before now. We'd had sex. Three times, actually. I'd seen his body in all his glorious nakedness, but this was different.

He was sprawled out on the bed hugging a pillow. My pillow. My own fault. I'd gotten up to go to the bathroom and returned to find that I'd been replaced. Seeing him completely nude, his huge, gorgeous body taking up most of the bed's real estate and that pillow clutched in his arms, he looked like a carefree, sated, sleepy god.

It was almost evening, and we'd had sex three times. Intense and eye-opening, slow while spooning, and finally hard and fast from behind. That last one was likely what had made me sore. I grinned. So worth it. I'd teased Dex with my mouth and hands, waking him much as he'd woken me. Seeing him all growly and fierce had been such a turn-on.

But it had also left me a little sore and longing for an Epsom bath. I wanted to head home and soak, preferably before Dex figured out exactly how tender I was. He'd feel bad, even though I'd practically screamed, "Fuck me harder."

Okay, I had screamed that.

But he'd still feel bad, because Dex was the kind of person who takes care of others. I would call it motherly but for the fact that the man had more testosterone than any five normal guys. A knight in shining armor with a dash of Betty Crocker and a pinch of Florence Nightingale.

Hmm. That didn't really fit either. There was nothing Betty or Florence about the massive hot man I was drooling over.

He was bossy in bed, but not out of it.

He was an amazing baker but hadn't used his

skills to woo me, only to cheer me up when I'd been down.

He was athletic and fit, but not obsessively so. In other words, my perfect workout partner.

He could laugh at himself, and when he laughed at others, it was with a kind heart.

He was sexy and kind and generous. He sent the best texts, made love like it was his job, and seemed to always know the right thing to say.

God. It was so fucking obvious I was in love with him. How hadn't I seen it happening?

I needed to process all of that. Because it was huge and I was the kind of person who needed to think about everything in the quiet of a safe space.

Also, I needed that Epsom bath, because we were definitely having more sex. Lots more sex. We were having all the sex.

Maybe there wasn't all that much processing to do.

Except the part where I freaked out about whether he felt the same way. Yeah, that would require some "processing." Aka, obsessing over.

I didn't want to wake him up, because then he would insist on walking me home, and if he did that, he'd see how sore I was. I wanted to avoid that if possible.

Texting was out, because I was pretty sure it would wake him and that defeated the purpose. I was sneaking out.

I finally landed on the old-fashioned option of a note on the kitchen table.

After dithering for a bit—because I didn't want to be needy or clingy or come on too strong, but I also didn't want him to feel like I'd *sneaked out* sneaked out—I finally landed on:

Ran home to clean up a bit. Didn't want to wake you. Want to come over for dinner?

I added a heart in front of my name. That wasn't like signing a note with the actual word "love," just implied a level of affection greater than friends. Maybe. I hoped.

Chelsea dogged my steps from the moment I left the bedroom till I stepped out the front door. I'd have sworn that dog was trying to guilt-trip me. She just didn't get the nuance of the situation. My lady parts needed some love if they were going to get any more loving. Also, I needed to go somewhere where I could openly freak out and act like the neurotic freak that I was.

I petted her tawny fur, and she wagged her tail and grinned at me.

Such a happy dog. Yeah, I'd be happy too if I

lived with the sexiest, kindest, most generous man alive.

Shit.

I had fallen so hard.

Time to exit the warm embrace of Dex's homey house, which included the company of both a loveable dog and an even more loveable dragon.

It was a quick walk back to my house. A few houses on Dex's street, including Mathilde's house, and a half dozen or so on mine and I'd be home.

Funny thing, I could see a faint glow around Mathilde's house. I'd certainly never noticed that before.

Wow, the neighbors kitty-corner to her had some crazy stuff growing in their yard. Like moonbeams with pink streaks.

I stopped and looked around me. The world had shifted. All around me were signs of magic. Some subtle, like the hazy glow that I could barely discern surrounding Mathilde's house, and some less so, like the moonbeams shooting up from the ground in the yard of what was otherwise a drab house.

It was...frightening? No. I examined my feelings and discovered that it wasn't actually. Not really. It was definitely interesting. I could stand here, spin in a circle, and see an entirely fresh panorama. The familiar landscape of my neighborhood had become new all over again.

As I stood frozen in place, staring at the newly revealed sights around me, I decided that the strongest emotion I felt was relief.

This was my world. *This* was what I'd seen as a little girl, and it was beautiful.

As I was contemplating whether my newly discovered feelings for Dex had something to do with the return of magic to my life, a dark SUV with tinted windows pulled up next to me.

Okay, so maybe I still didn't like the idea of people thinking I was weird. If someone popped their head out and asked me if I was okay, I refused to be held responsible for my actions.

The window rolled down, and instead of questioning the state of my mental health or—the much more likely scenario—asking me for directions, the man in the passenger seat asked very politely, "Are you Kaylee Roze?"

And since my life had been, up to this point, filled with innocuous people going about their innocuous days, I didn't think twice before responding, "Hi, yes, that's me. How can I help you?"

He didn't answer. He and the two men who

exited from the back seat were too busy surrounding me and then hustling me to the back of the SUV.

I was zip-tied, gagged, and stuffed under a blanket before I could do more than claim they'd made a mistake. Obviously, they had the wrong Kaylee Roze.

They didn't say a word, not after the one man asked me to confirm my identity.

On the plus side, I did have a small amount of information about them. They were all some sort of magical being. It had been so long since I'd seen magic, and I'd hardly had the opportunity as a child to put a label on what I had seen, but they didn't appear to be particularly powerful magical beings... probably?

In any event, they hadn't glowed all that much, so I was taking that as indication that they were magical but didn't have that much magic or it wasn't an especially powerful sort of magic.

On the negative side, whether they had magic or not, they definitely had guns.

But again in the plus column, my neighborhood was really quiet and had its share of window-watchers. The three men who'd bundled me up and stowed me like luggage had been fast, but there was a chance that someone had witnessed my abduction and called the police. Hell, if the witness was Ralph Sanchez, he'd have gotten the damn plate number. I always thought Ralph was paranoid, writing all those license plate numbers down, but I had a new appreciation for his diligence.

At some point, I realized that I probably should have been paying attention to my surroundings. Almost any character in one of my books would have done a much better job of picking up clues. Unfortunately, the men in the car didn't talk at all. No name dropping, no revealing of ulterior motives. Not even a discussion of dinner options.

Dammit, now I was hungry. Dex and I had skipped lunch.

Oh, hell. Dex would be worried when I didn't get in touch about dinner.

And that led down another train of thought. Could dragons track people like bloodhounds? Were they bulletproof? And what exactly had Dex meant when he'd told me he couldn't shift? He was a dragon who couldn't turn into a dragon. That did seem problematic, but then—was it really? We could hardly have dragons flying around in the sky willy-nilly.

Damn. We hadn't had time to talk about any of this. We'd been too busy getting busy.

Not that I regretted that. At all.

It would just be nice to have information about him and his dragon buddies. And yes, I had finally figured out what dragon sex was. Bain and Archer were obviously dragons, as well, and Taylor was clearly getting laid on the regular by her very own dragon.

I had no clue how long it would take Dex to realize I was gone, no clue if he could find me even if he did notice I was missing, and not the faintest idea if I even wanted him near these guys with guns if he did manage to figure out where I was.

Also, how the fuck was I not freaking out right now?

For years, the mere mention of magic put me in a tizzy. Now, I'm all, "Magical dudes with guns." Shrug. No problem?

We came to a stop, and I was still freaking out that I wasn't freaking out. I was neurotic. Fragile. Not equipped to deal with men with guns.

And my emotional response was, basically, whatevs.

Maybe this was what a mental breakdown felt like.

Huh. If so, I definitely should have had one years ago.

I woke up and Kaylee was gone.

I had a bad feeling in my gut, and Chelsea didn't look pleased by her absence, but then I'd found her note.

She was cooking me dinner. I smiled.

I knew some random facts about her life (that her mother was a war demon, for one) and some of her preferences (sweaters that felt like cuddly blankets, wool socks when it was only sixty degrees outside, and that she loved hearing how much I loved her tits), but I didn't happen to know if she could cook.

I hunted down my phone and sent a quick text.

What time are you thinking?

She didn't reply right away. Since I was guessing

she was in the shower, I went ahead and asked about logistics. She'd see it when she was done shampooing her hair and shaving her legs—or whatever she was doing in the shower. And now I was half-hard.

I shook my head and typed out: *I've got crème brûlée. Should I order takeout?*

Then I set my phone aside and grabbed a shower myself.

Since I kept thinking about berry nipples I wanted to suck and the wet soapy sheen of Kaylee's skin while she took a shower, I had to tug one out. It barely took the edge off.

I wanted her. She was my mate. I wanted to fuck her until she was round with my baby. I also wanted to watch her come and hear her chant my name like she was worshipping me. Or my cock. Either way.

And I was rock hard again.

I grabbed my phone to see if she'd replied to my earlier texts, but there was nothing.

I dressed, checked my phone again, and then decided I wasn't the worst person alive if I stopped by her house. I wasn't exactly unannounced. I'd been invited.

"Come on, Chelsea." If Kaylee didn't want her in the house, I could run her back home, but I didn't think she'd mind. I knew she had a cleaning service, and they'd catch any hair that Chels left behind.

It was easier to have her at Kaylee's, in case we decided to sleep over at her place. Because, yes, I did let my dick make a few decisions for me, and one of them was that I'd rather be in bed longer with Kaylee than have to run home multiple times to feed and potty Chelsea.

Five minutes later, I was at Kaylee's house—but Kaylee wasn't. Her car was in the garage, the house was locked up tight, and she wasn't inside.

I knew this, because I'd broken in. Like Archer had said, was it really breaking in if it was so easy? Also, I was buying my woman new locks. And a security system. And one of those surveillance camera things that hooked up to a phone. My phone.

I was overreacting. I knew it, but that didn't ease the frantic feeling building inside me. The cool air lifting my wings and sunning on hot rocks wasn't going anywhere near my level of anxiety right now. Meditation could go fuck itself.

Where could she be?

Walking? Since we'd jogged this morning and we'd had sex three times since, I didn't see her opting to take a walk.

At a neighbor's? Hell, Mathilde. Mathilde's house was on her way home.

I called Mathilde. Kaylee wasn't there, and now Mathilde was worried about her, as well. That couldn't be good, because the incompetent witch loved Kaylee and might try to do magic to locate her. But I'd been frantic and too worried about Kaylee to take the time to make sure she didn't do something so foolish.

"Fucking pick up the fucking phone, you —Bain?"

"What the hell is wrong with you?" Bain must have caught some of my rant.

"Kaylee's missing."

"Where are you?"

"Her house."

"We're on the way." And he hung up.

I didn't need to ask who he meant. He'd make sure Archer came.

Ten minutes later, Taylor showed up at the door. "The idiots are at your house, raiding your closet. They didn't bring any clothes."

They'd flown. Of course they had, because this was an emergency and they *could* fly. They could fly, they could cloak, and they could throw fire.

She bent down to pet Chelsea who'd been

whining intermittently and pacing. "You sweet, sweet girl. We'll find her. Don't worry."

We better. And this better have nothing to do with the bullshit brewing in the shifter community lately. No one had any respect for dragons these days. Let a few decades pass without torching a small town or a major event and the world forgot about you.

"Come on." Taylor gestured that I should follow her. When I hesitated, she said, "You've looked everywhere in the house. There's no note. No sign of break-in or a struggle."

Except where I'd broken in, that was all true. She was right; there wasn't any reason to stay here. I followed her out the door, thumb-locking it as I went since I didn't have a key.

I fell into step next to her. She was moving at a good clip.

"You've called Maddie?" When I didn't reply, she prompted, "Van Helsing. The PI Kaylee hired to find her mother."

"I haven't. How did you even know about that?" I couldn't remember if I'd told Bain, but I didn't think I'd mentioned it. That was Kaylee's private business.

"Oh, honey. The world of magic is kinda small. It's like a high school clique."

Shifters, vamps, monsters, monster-hunters, demons...not small. We also didn't all mingle. Mostly we made efforts *not* to mingle.

I shook my head as I dialed Maddie Van Helsing. I only had her number on my phone because Kaylee had hired her. Not a small clique.

"You've reached Leila, Maddie's assistant. What do you want?"

Madeleine had her calls forwarded? I didn't have time for this shit. "This is Dexter Brodie." I used my growly, angry dragon voice. "Kaylee's missing. I need to speak to Madeleine immediately."

"You sure Kaylee wants to be found, big guy?"

"She's my mate."

Taylor would have fallen over her own feet if I hadn't steadied her with my free hand.

"Well, hell. She's out of cell service for the next few hours. Does it have anything to do with those rat shifters you pissed off?"

"Wrong dragon, and I can't see how." But I did make note to ask Bain, the right dragon, if he could check on that.

"Okay." She huffed out a loud breath. "Well, shit. I could give two fucks about you and your personal drama, but Maddie'll be pissed that she wasn't available to help Kaylee. I'm forwarding you her sister's number. Call her. She'll help. I'll sort it with the Guild."

My phone pinged with a text just before Leila hung up on me.

Before today, I would have said no way in hell I was calling a Van Helsing for help, but—maybe. I was desperate. There weren't any leads, and I knew —in my gut, I knew—that she was in trouble.

I checked the text as we arrived at my house. "Mia Van Helsing," I read aloud.

"Oh," Taylor said with too much enthusiasm. "I hear she's got lady balls like diamonds. You should definitely call her."

"Who's he calling, babe?" Bain asked.

"Maddie's out of the office, so Leila sent Mia's number. Said she'd sort it with the Monster Hunter Guild so she can take a private case."

How did Taylor know so much about this life after being mated less than a year to Bain?

And I wasn't yelling at her, because she didn't deserve it, but I didn't want to call a fucking Van Helsing, even if I should because I couldn't fucking shift.

"Hon," Bain said in a gentle voice, "why don't you head to the kitchen and see if you can make some dinner."

"Got it." She touched my arm, and I realized my hands were balled into fists. "We're going to find her." Then she squeezed my arm and left.

Once she was on the other side of the house, I let loose. "Fucking hell. Just...fuuuck!"

"Yeah," Archer said as he joined us from the back of the house. He was pulling on one of my long-sleeve T-shirts. It was black. He'd also borrowed black sweats. "You're not gonna like this, but I think we should call the mother."

My chest was tight, my brain spinning. I couldn't think like this. I hadn't thought to call Maddie. Taylor had reminded me. And now this. It hadn't even occurred to me to call Lizbet Jones. Shit, and I'd forgotten about the rat shifters.

I mentioned it now, but Bain dismissed it as highly improbable. He still sent a few texts. He had contacts within their community.

And I did nothing. I was fucking useless.

I hadn't been this fucked in the head since...

Not in a long, long time.

There was one thing I needed to do.

"I'm..." The words *emotionally compromised* were on the tip of my tongue.

Bain and Archer waited. Each willing to lay down his life for me, I knew. This might be harder.

"Kaylee's my mate." Neither man looked surprised. "I'm not myself. I can't shift, and I'm not sure I trust my judgment right now. I need you to help me keep my head straight."

It killed me to say it. But I'd been here before, with someone I loved, who couldn't defend themselves, in danger. And I'd made bad choices then.

Archer took a step closer, looked me in the eyes, and then smacked me. An openhanded slap to the face.

It surprised the hell out of me, but also—"What the fuck?"

"If you're going to act like a hysterical bitch, then I'm going to smack you like one."

Bain cocked his head, like he agreed but wouldn't have said it that way.

"What is wrong with you two? My woman—"

"Your mate," Bain corrected.

"My mate," I growled, "is missing. You both know what happened last time."

"Last time," Bain said as if he didn't see the connection. He was blind, because it was crystal clear. "Last time when you were barely more than a teenager and faced five older, more experienced fighters. And lived."

"My brother didn't."

Bain crossed his arms. "Yeah, and your parents were too grief stricken to admit they'd coddled him and failed in his training. You survived. Instead of loving the son they had, they grieved the one they lost. They weren't perfect people, but..."

"They fucked up," Archer said. "Badly."

Had they? I'd lived. Robert had died. They were allowed to grieve.

But they'd also let me believe I was partially at fault for Robert's death. That my living was the ultimate insult.

Maybe I had been responsible, maybe not. But just like Archer's broken heart, it had all happened a long fucking time ago. I'd lived lifetimes since then.

"You're worried for your woman." Bain didn't look like a complete asshole, and yet, he said stupid, obvious shit.

"Yes," I agreed, when he didn't say anything else. "I have no fire, no claws, no fangs. I have no idea where she is, and I'm fucking useless to help her."

"For a guy who's usually known for his chill, you seriously have none." Archer looked ready to give me another smack.

I glared at him, daring him to lay a hand on me. I had no fire, but I could fight.

He arched an eyebrow. "I think what Bain was

getting around to saying is that you are not useless. You can fight, you have us as backup, and you have your mate—who's the daughter of a fucking war demon."

"She is," I agreed. "I'm not sure what that means. She's repressed her magic for so long I'm not sure she can use it, or what she can do with it. We need to find her." I rubbed my jaw. "I'll call Lizbet. Who's got Mia?"

Archer volunteered, so I forwarded the number Leila had provided.

I texted Maddie's number with a request for Lizbet's contact details, hoping that Leila would see the message. If I didn't hear from her quickly, I'd—

My phone pinged with a text. No message was included, just a number.

I took Chelsea with me in the backyard. I hated to admit it, but on top of being worried about Kaylee's safety, I was also worried she'd kick me in the shins when she found out I called her mother.

I scrubbed a hand across my face. I'd rather my woman be angry with me and safe, than otherwise, so I dialed the number.

After two rings, a woman's voice said, "Dexter Brodie."

Demons loved power. And they liked manipulating people. Playing games. Toying with humanity and any being they considered lesser than themselves.

I had no idea how she knew I'd be calling, and my number was unlisted. But it was almost certainly part of a game to her.

"Lizbet." Demons went by their first names, because the last was always false. I'd try to avoid asking a direct question, if possible, instead sticking with statements of fact. "Kaylee's missing."

"Poor little bound dragon. Have you misplaced your favorite toy?" Unlike her words, her tone was businesslike.

"I've misplaced your daughter." I was a big enough person to accept blame, if that encouraged the demon to talk.

"Hmm." She paused then continued in the same brisk tone. "She's not missing or misplaced."

This was her daughter she was speaking of. Her own flesh and blood. I swallowed my distaste, focusing instead on the implication Lizbet laid forth: she knew where Kaylee was right now.

"But *I* don't know where she is."

For the first time, her tone was sharp. "I do think you should keep a closer eye on your toys. Especially your favorites."

Maybe she did care for her child's welfare after all.

"I will." And that wasn't a lie. I wasn't Kaylee's keeper, but once we were mated, I would more easily be able to find her if she was distressed or in danger. A soul connection was useful in such instances.

"The lizards have her. They want a concession on a contract and thought to use her as leverage. I've refused."

My blood boiled.

She. Refused.

Simple as that.

Only the sharp nudge of Chelsea's narrow, cold nose against my hand kept me from saying something regrettable.

Kaylee could be dead already. No, I'd know that, even without the mating bond. Surely I'd know that. But she could be hurt. Whoever they were, the people who had her were goons, all muscle and no finesse, to have thought such a strategy would work. Fuck. They might have cut off one of her fingers. Or worse.

I couldn't help it. I had to ask. Mia could likely find the location, but this would be faster. Time was precious. "Do you know where they're keeping her?"

She laughed. "Foolish dragon. You think you'll

save her. She doesn't need saving. She will fell her foes with a click of her half-war-demon fingers."

Only after Lizbet ended the call did her words translate to their true meaning. She knew Kaylee had magic. She must have always known. Why did she leave her with her father? Untrained, unprepared to wield her magic?

I didn't believe for a second that Kaylee could "fell her foes." That was Lizbet's ego talking. I spun around and ran back into the house, straight to the living room.

Bain and Archer were both on the phone; Taylor was on her laptop.

"Lizbet claims the lizards have her."

Archer muted his phone. "She has to mean the crocs. They're new in the area, and they've been causing some problems. They'd also hate being called lizards."

"It's something to do with a contract negotiation between Lizbet and these lizards." I wasn't convinced the crocs were the right choice. Goons, yes, but unlikely to be doing business with Lizbet.

"Oh, oh, oh." Taylor was waving her hand in the air and hopping in her seat on the sofa.

"Just tell us, hon." Bain had already ended the

call he'd been on, but now he moved to sit next to Taylor.

"I looked up Lizbet Jones, and she's brokering a deal between two software companies. Could it be related to that? Are there lizards involved with this software deal?"

Bain sighed. "Komodos."

"Assholes," Archer snapped. He returned to his phone call only to end it.

"I'll kill them." Happily. Without regret.

"You can't." Bain held up his hands. "But you can maim them, and I'll help."

"We both will," Archer agreed.

Taylor's head bounced between us. "You know these Komodos?"

We all said, "Yes," with equal amounts of disdain.

Bain scowled. "They're the *other* dragons. The kind that can't fly, have no fire, and like to use guns. In other words, not really dragons. Lizards."

"What the heck? Aren't they from some island in Indonesia?" Taylor asked.

"Maybe once," Archer said. "Now they're from New Jersey."

"New Jersey," she repeated it like it wasn't believable. Everyone was from somewhere, and Komodos were from Jersey. For the last few centuries.

"I'm calling Mia." Archer lifted his phone. "She's got a screw loose, but I bet she can get us an address faster than my people for wherever it is the Komodos conduct their shadier activities in Austin."

We'd find Kaylee.

And when we did, she'd be alive and in one piece, because contemplating anything else made me heartsick.

And then the two of us were completing the mating ritual, binding us soul to soul for the rest of our lives.

If she agreed.

She better fucking agree.

I wasn't even going to pretend to be chill about that.

KAYLEE

One of the men seemed a little nicer than the others, and he said, "We just need something from your mother. When she delivers, you can go home."

Which was when I figured out he was probably worried about what my mother would do to him, prompting him to be more careful with me. Either way, it was more information than I was getting from the other two.

They'd snatched me from the back of the SUV and hauled me into an office. There wasn't anyone around to see, because they'd parked the SUV inside the warehouse.

That was where we were. In a generic warehouse, probably in the middle of nowhere, where no one was ever going to find me.

Hopefully, my mother would agree to whatever it was these men wanted, and hopefully they wouldn't then decide to kill me.

Or maybe dragons did have bloodhound-like qualities and Dex would find me.

If he even realized I was missing.

He could still be asleep. Without a watch or cell phone, I didn't have a good feel for how much time had passed. An hour? More?

Two of the four men came back looking grim. They weren't tied to a chair, so they could take that attitude and shove it up their asses. My hands were falling asleep even as I continued to move my fingers to keep the blood flow moving, my shoulders hurt from having my hands tied behind me, and my vagina was angry it missed out on that Epsom salt bath.

In short, I was not happy.

I came close to pointing out that between the kidnapping and the blackmail, these yahoos were looking at two felonies. I managed to restrain myself.

Wow. Look at me. A bunch of thugs with guns kidnapped me, and I had to rein in the sass. Who'd have thought that would be my reaction? Not me. Not a month ago. Hell, not even a week ago.

But fuck them. My mom was a war demon. I was the daughter of a fucking war demon.

Reality settled in a split second later, because it seemed that being the daughter of a war demon meant that I could see all the magic in the world. Even more than other magical people.

Period.

Not to say that I was disappointed by that fact, because seeing magic in Dex's dog when he couldn't was pretty cool. But it wasn't exactly a useful skill when faced with violent thugs.

I wasn't liking the look the two shared. And the one guy was carrying a pair of bolt cutters. There weren't any chains around. Or locks. Shit.

"My boyfriend's a dragon." It just sort of came out.

These guys had some magic, so they had to believe in dragons, and dragons were scary...right?

"A dragon? Yeah, okay. Whatever, lady."

"You don't believe in dragons?"

He saw the confused look on my face and smirked. "What? Like that they exist? Of course. That you're dating one? Whatever. I don't care. What the hell is he going to do to us? They're the Boy

Scouts of the shifter world. Who's scared of dragons?"

While it was reassuring to hear that Dex and his friends weren't known as the underworld thugs of the magical world, it seemed a little odd that huge fire-breathing animals didn't elicit even a twinge of concern.

Maybe they were little dragons?

The guy without the bolt cutters moved to cut my hands loose. He was careful not to hurt me, which was reassuring. Maybe I'd read this situation wrong.

But then he grabbed my hand and forced it onto the desk. Not wrong. Not wrong at all. These two thugs were going to cut one of my fingers off.

A funny thing happened.

I got mad.

Really fucking mad.

Like, lop-a-guy's-head-off mad.

Like, eviscerate-a-sorry-kidnapping-bastard mad.

Like...

Grab all the magic, all of it, because I couldn't just see it. I could feel it. Taste it.

Grab all the magic, and make it my bitch.

That kind of mad.

There was some screaming.

I ignored it.

I yanked that magic like a carpet from under their feet.

Or not.

Because I could feel it pulsing in my veins.

Fuck. Maybe more like a vampire chugging blood.

I opened my eyes. I hadn't even realized I'd closed them.

The two who were about to cut off one of my fingers were limp heaps of man-thugs on the ground.

I was still tied to the chair.

And, actually, I didn't know if the finger-stealing asses were dead or passed out, but if they happened to still be alive, or if their friends were, I needed to get gone now. I had no clue how I'd done what I'd just done. I didn't even know *what* I'd done.

I grabbed the knife on the desk, the same one used to cut my hands free, and sliced the zip ties binding my ankles to the chair legs.

Standing was harder.

I had pins and needles in my feet and halfway up my legs. Also, I had this weird bubbly sensation that made me sort of want to laugh but also smash something.

Was I high? Is this what it felt like to get high?

It was weird.

I looked for a phone in the office, because I was pretty sure Dex would know what to do in this situation. Also, we'd just had tons of sex. Pretty sure he was good for a ride. Calling a rideshare seemed iffy in this scenario.

Holy shit, I felt weird.

There wasn't a phone, so I weighed the risks of leaving the office and maybe finding one of those other guys against the risk of the guys in the office waking up really, really angry. Since I was pretty sure I saw one of them breathing, I decided to venture out of the office and away from the men I'd knocked out. They weren't gonna be happy when they woke up.

I opened the door to the office and half a second later a knight in shining armor busted through the warehouse door.

I really was high, wasn't I?

Because when I squinted and tried to see through all the shining light, I could discern that the man standing there wasn't a knight. It was Dex— with a sword in his hand. And a gun in his other hand. Who knew that he was ambidextrous? Not me.

He shone with the purest of lights. And glints of fire. Oh yeah, there was definitely fire.

But in my defense, what with the shining light and the sword he was carrying, he really did look like a knight.

No, scratch that.

With the beard and the fire in his eyes, he looked like a demented modern-day Viking.

He had lost all of his chill.

Completely.

Utterly.

It was... Wow, it was sexy as fuck.

He looked like he wanted to break some necks and bury some bodies, but only after he'd bathed in his enemies' blood.

That should have freaked me the fuck out.

But it didn't.

It made me wet. And horny.

Oh my God, was that boy getting some later.

And then the most wondrous event of my life happened.

I saw my very first dragon.

s we closed in on the location Mia had provided, there was a great sucking pull.

A great sucking *magical* pull.

My hex broke.

Just like that. Gone. Like chains had snapped and fallen away.

My dragon was free.

I was currently being carried, like a preflight infant, in Bain's claws, so I couldn't shift. I also happened to be carrying clothes for both Archer and Bain. Those fuckers weren't going anywhere near Kaylee without clothes.

"Was that...?" Archer didn't finish the question.

Because none of us knew anything. Not until we landed at the warehouse location Mia had given us.

That magical implosion we'd all felt came from there.

Dragon flight defied physics, but it still took time. The last minutes before we landed were fraught.

We didn't know what we'd find. For all we knew, Lizbet got her panties in a twist and decided to rain hell down on her blackmailers.

But that didn't explain my hex breaking.

Bain released me a foot from the ground then landed. I threw the pack I'd carried for him and Archer on the ground, but only after drawing my sword.

Sword in one hand, gun in the other, I was ready for lizard or human. And I wasn't waiting. Bain and Archer would catch up. I needed in that warehouse *now*. In case Lizbet had lost her mind or—

I didn't stop to consider various permutations. That magical implosion meant something, and it had happened a good two and a half minutes previous.

I busted through the door to find...

Two men on the ground.

And Kaylee.

At the head of a set of stairs, directly in front of a door, looking alive and whole. She looked amazing.

Her fluffy sweater had been lost, and she was

wearing nothing but a T-shirt and jeans, but she looked magnificent. Her hair was pulled back, her posture tall and proud. She looked ready to kick some ass. My guess, she'd been the source of that magical bomb, and her mom had been exactly right. She could take care of herself.

I couldn't be prouder.

I felt an uncontrollable need to shift. I'd been half of myself ever since I'd met her, and now that I was whole, I was desperate to spread my wings, flash my iridescent underbelly, fry some assholes with my fire.

No sooner had I thought it than I was winged, scaled, fanged, and clawed.

There was room in the warehouse. It was nothing more than an open space.

Kaylee squealed. Like a kid who's seen their first unicorn...or their first dragon.

I arched my neck, displaying my prettiest scales, the ones under my chin, and spread my wings.

She scrambled down the stairs, running until she stood directly in front of me. "Can you talk when you're all...dragon-y?"

I laughed, and her eyes widened.

"You sound...the same."

"It's magic." I flexed my wings. "The same for

flight. My wings control my direction of travel. They don't give me the ability to fly."

"Amazing." She was stroking my neck. I don't think she even realized she was doing it, but I flexed under her fingertips anyway. "So soft. I wouldn't have thought they'd be soft. And all the colors!" Her fingers moved from the dark blue-green scales on the top of my neck to the iridescent, multicolored scales underneath.

"Uh-hm." Her fingers felt so good on my neck. A rumble started low in my belly and traveled through my body. It didn't waiver as I watched Bain and Archer in their clothed human forms secure the two men on the warehouse floor.

"You're purring," she whispered, as if speaking too loud would make me stop.

After a few minutes, she stopped rubbing my neck and said, "Dex. I think you have a PR problem. And since I'm the other half of you—" My heart thrummed loudly in my chest. She wasn't talking about mating. She didn't even know what a dragon's mate was. Even so... "—that means *we* have a PR problem."

Much as I would have preferred she keep stroking my scales, or even better yet, explain exactly what she meant when she said she was the other half of me—was it a casual comment, or did she feel what I felt?—I deferred to her wishes that we discuss this public relations issue. "Tell me what you're thinking."

And she did. It was the same bullshit that Bain had dealt with. No one respected dragons any more. Because we showed restraint, they assumed we wouldn't protect our own.

I remained in my dragon form, because if I shifted back to my human form, I'd be all over her. The need to mark her was even more intense than it had been when we'd been intimate.

"So, any ideas?" Kaylee asked.

I felt a pulse of guilt. I'd been paying attention. Mostly.

Bain and Archer had secured two additional men who'd been in the office with Kaylee, but they were back now and listening.

"Easy," Archer said. "Kill the kidnappers. They should expect as much. Probably sent their disposable guys to do the dirty work."

"Uh, no." Kaylee's hand was still on my neck, but she stopped petting me at the mention of murder.

"We torch the place," Bain announced. "It's showy. They'll take a multimillion-dollar hit on the property loss."

"But, what about the other properties? Or if the fire gets out of control and someone's hurt?"

I rubbed my jaw against her shoulder. "Magical fire. No one's hurt, because it's out before the human firefighters show up. And unlike physical fire, we control it until it's extinguished."

Bain winced. "Mostly."

Kaylee latched on to his comment. "What do you mean mostly? Can you guarantee no one will be hurt or not?"

"I can," I promised. And I proved it to her.

Kaylee got her first dragon flight, and she got to watch me light up the warehouse where she'd been held captive and threatened.

It was a feel-good moment watching it burn. Like playing with puppies. Especially since Bain would have his rat shifter contacts spread the word that it was dragon retaliation for acts against a dragon mate.

It was the twenty-first century. We shouldn't have to rely on intimidation and showy acts of destruction. But Kaylee was right. We did have a PR problem. And if a little fire kept our mates safe, I was completely fine with some light destruction of property.

I was thankful that Kaylee had handled her

captors, because I was certain if I had, I'd have removed their heads. She would not have approved.

Also, she'd needed the confidence boost of handling herself in a dangerous situation, and I'd gained the comfort of knowing my mate was a complete badass.

Not that I wasn't capable of protecting her. I was.

My brother's death was a very long time ago. Many lifetimes. I needed to let that pain go, and along with it, the guilt.

I had a future to forge.

With my mate.

KAYLEE

It had been days since Dex had explained the concept of dragon mates.

Binding of souls, shared life force, yada ya.

I loved him, a fact of which he was well aware, since apparently I'd gone from chanting his name when I came to chanting "I love you" over and over again.

He loved me, a fact of which I was well aware, because he told me so, and I trusted Dex.

So...what the fuck? When did this whole mating thing happen?

Not one to dally when important matters needed doing, I called Taylor and got the basic details.

I was ready for sexy dragon biting action.

I had slutty-hot lingerie. I had a horny dragon. This was happening.

Dex had gone to get groceries, because, unlike Archer, he knew how to grocery shop for himself. He tried to convince me to go with him, but that didn't fit with the plan.

When I heard the garage door opening, I apologized profusely to Chelsea and put her in the guest room she stayed in when Dex and I were getting our freak on outside of the bedroom. Kitchen sex? Great. Living room couch sex? Very nice. Laundry room sex? Surprisingly awesome.

I had on my sexy teddy. Dex's favorite color, blue, of course. Not that I was saying he was egotistical, but I managed to find one that had just a hint of green shining through...like his gorgeous mostly blue but green-tinged top scales.

My thighs were damp from the excitement coursing through me. Practically living with the walking epitome of sex meant that I was always turned on, but this was different.

"Hey, Kaylee, hon? What's going on?"

I'd turned off all the lights and lit a few candles, because that was romantic, right?

Dex flicked on the kitchen light. His arms were full of perishables.

Dammit. Maybe I didn't think this all the way through.

But Dex took one look at me and dumped everything on the counter. His nostrils flared and his eyes glinted with the fire I could always see in him.

I'd learned to dial down my magical sight so it wasn't distracting, but I knew exactly what Dex looked like in all his magical glory. He was my knight is shining scales.

"That's new." His eyes told me how much he appreciated the teddy.

"Don't you want to put the milk away?"

"Nope." He stepped closer, his eyes flaring with passion.

"Or the, ah..." I glanced at the counter. "Cheese?"

"Uh-uh." He was outright stalking me now as I moved toward the bedroom.

Then I ran.

Because dragons *loved* to chase.

I could hear his sexy growl behind me. He could have caught me, but he waited until we made it to the bedroom. Then he tackled me.

Exactly as I planned.

I arched my back, snuggling my ass into his hard cock.

Taylor had told me that dragon mating required

a certain position. I was just giving my dragon the hint.

He covered me chest to back, his cock nestled between my butt cheeks.

I lifted my ass, and he gave me enough room to get to my knees. His big hands shaped and squeezed my ass. He was about to find my special surprise.

"Fuck, yes." His fingers sunk inside me.

Crotchless teddy for the win.

He thrust two fingers in and out, teasing me, knowing I wanted him. His hard length pushing inside me. He knew I was ready for him. I was dripping wet, wanting. I moaned, and he added a third finger.

I thrust back against his fingers, hungry for more and a little pissed that he wasn't fucking me.

Reaching behind me, I squeezed his hard length.

His fingers disappeared, and I reached down to play with myself while he stripped.

He came back seconds later and smacked my hand away. "Mine."

I sunk into the bed. I fucking loved it when he got all growly and possessive.

And he knew it. He grasped the back of my neck with one hand and lifted my ass higher with the other. I was splayed out, waiting for him to fuck me.

He didn't. He teased me with the fat head of his cock, and I started to beg.

"You want me?" he grumbled

"Yes, yes, yes. I want you. I love you, Dex. I love you. Fuck me."

And only then did he thrust inside me.

I made some more noises, probably screamed, probably cried, because it was so good. Each thrust made me feel *everything*. It was so good. So hard. So good. I love you, Dex. Fuck me, Dex. Harder, Dex. Yes, yes, yes. Fuck! Bite me, Dex. Please, please. Mark me. Mate me. Fuck me. Yes.

At some point, I realized I was saying all that out loud. And that was fine, because I didn't have any secrets from Dex.

I loved him. So much.

And that was when I felt it. The magic. The fire. The bite.

My heart was open. My heart was his.

His mating fangs sank into my neck and I screamed as I came.

Dex pumped inside me four more times, five, and then he collapsed on top of me, whispering, "I love you, Kaylee."

EPILOGUE, WAR DEMONS AS MOTHERS: KAYLEE

Dex had agreed to my meeting with my mother under threat of no sex.

To be fair, I said, "Either you agree to let me meet with my mother alone or I'm withholding sex." And then I immediately laughed. We both knew I wasn't about to withhold sex.

Because one, I loved having sex with my favorite nerdy-hot dragon.

And two, Dex wasn't the boss of me. I didn't need sex or the lack of to manipulate my mate.

I'd lived under my dad's benevolent tyranny for far too long. My dad and I were good. I understood why he'd done the things he had, but I wasn't about to let anyone else run my life again. Not even a hot dragon. Not even my mate.

That said, I didn't want Dex worrying. So I'd arm-twisted him to agree to come with me, wait in the lobby, then take me to lunch afterwards. But I'd also made him promise he wouldn't try to bust into our meeting and take down my demon mother.

Now that he was all dragony again, he was really full of himself.

But let's be real, he wasn't capable of taking on a war demon by himself.

When I said as much to him, his reply had been, "Of course not. I've got you to help me."

True statement. I was on his side every time.

But me and Dex against my mother was an eventuality that would inevitably lead to years and years of therapy.

When I pointed this out to Dex, he pouted, then agreed to stay in the lobby.

And that was how I rolled these days. Point to me.

So here I was, in my mother's massive corner office, on the top floor, asking her all the good stuff. Like...

"What exactly is a war demon?"

She laughed. It was a throaty sound, full of the deep sort of pleasure I associated with the truly uninhibited.

"It's an old-fashioned name. I used to use the weather to attack my prey—or my enemies." She shrugged. "Mostly, these days, I sit in a boardroom and decimate men with small minds. It's more fun. Less fallout." She wrinkled her nose. "Certainly less cleanup. Everyone's so fussy these days about visible magic."

Uh, my mom was kind of a badass. And maybe a murderer. I might be conflicted. Which was fine. She did give birth to me and let me stay with my dad even though she knew I had magic. (Yeah, figured that one finally.) And there was the trust fund. It would be something nice for my kids, if nothing else. But on the flip side, she had left me to fend for myself against a bunch of poisonous lizard men who liked to use guns.

And moving right along. Now was not the time to unpack all *that*.

"So, do you have a bunch of kids?" Because I wanted to know if I had any half siblings running around. Seemed like the sort of information one should know about one's family. Probably.

"Not really. Demons aren't very fertile." She shrugged with one shoulder, as if she didn't really care. "The last was, oh, three hundred years ago? Maybe four hundred."

What the hell? So, Mom was ancient, and also, I probably didn't have a ton of secret siblings.

I nodded casually, like it was no big deal that the woman who'd given birth to me had lived through more than a handful of centuries.

"Look. I'm not motherly. I'm not maternal. I'm not the sort of person who calls on birthdays—or ever really. That's why your father raised you. He's —" She pressed her lips together, then almost reluctantly said, "He's a good man."

What? What had just happened? A demon being sort of...human?

I reined in my shock long enough to deliver the message that was the real reason behind this meeting. Not that I didn't want to pick her brain, but that wasn't actually why I'd come.

"That's all good. Let's be real here."

She arched an eyebrow at me. "Do, let's."

"I'm here to make sure you're not planning to cause any problems for my dad, my mate, or his friends."

"Why would I do that?" she asked, as if demons weren't known for being assholes just to be assholes.

I stared at her, expression completely blank.

Was that a twitch of her facial muscles near her lips? Was that a smile trying to break free?

I challenge Mommy Dearest about her intentions and she's fighting a smile. Hopefully that wasn't bad?

"I have no interest in dragons."

Whew. I just barely contained a visible expression of relief. "And my father?"

"Like I said, a good man. I hear he's married."

My eyes widened. My stepmother so wasn't up for any interaction with Lizbet. None at all. Lizbet would eat her alive, hair and bones included.

Then she did smile. "Stop. I sent a wedding gift. I wish them a long and happy marriage."

"Right. Excellent." And then I remembered my manners and added, "Thank you."

"Now that that business is done, what other questions do you have?"

I settled in to grill my mother about war demons, my magic, and anything else I thought she might share.

It was a fruitful hour.

But the hour afterward was even better.

Dex and I ended up skipping lunch. We had better things to do.

EPILOGUE, COFFEE SHOP CHAOS: KAYLEE

I shifted in my seat after I parked. I had a hint of lingering soreness. Not painful, just a tender reminder that Dex had sexed me up good this morning. We were going to have to have a chat about sexy time versus work time...eventually. Not yet. I was enjoying a slower pace with work. Why not take advantage of the flexibility my job provided?

The mild tenderness I was feeling would probably be gone by this evening. It better be. Dex was all about morning sex—hell, he was all about sex any time of day; my dragon was a machine—but I was more about evening sex. I didn't want my evening plans upset by a tender coochie.

I'd have to ask my neighbor if there was something magical that fixed sensitive lady parts. She was really embracing her witchy side again, now that she'd managed some magic that had the right sort of results: love everlasting, fated soul mates united, and all that.

I opened the car door, and the scent of roasting coffee hit me.

Taylor and I were finally meeting up with Susie. I asked Taylor to come a little early, but I'd expected to have to wait and was surprised when I found her already sitting at a table. She even had a drink.

"You will not believe this," I announced as I approached. I had big news. So big. I didn't want to tell her over the phone, and since we'd planned to meet today anyway, it had been the perfect opportunity. "I had lunch with my neighbor yesterday."

Taylor looked unimpressed with my revelation. Or distracted. She kept looking at the door. "And? I thought she came over most days."

"Mathilde comes over most days." I sat down. "Hazel came over yesterday." I waited for her to register my big-news tone.

Finally, she looked away from the door. "Wait, who's Hazel?"

"Exactly." I leaned close and lowered my voice. "She's Mathilde."

Taylor's nose wrinkled in displeasure. "I don't understand."

Which was weirdly satisfying, since I was constantly pedaling hard when it came to understanding her. But in this instance, I don't think anyone would pick up on the Mathilde-Hazel conundrum—not unless they had a freakishly long lifespan and created multiple identities for themselves.

"Check this out. Mathilde calls me, announces that Mrs. Franks has moved in with her son, who lives in Dallas, and then laughs like she's just announced the wicked witch had died."

"Who is Mrs. Franks?"

I had her full attention now. Which was good, because this was some confusing shit. "Mrs. Franks is *not* the wicked witch. She *is* the only person in the neighborhood who remembers what Mathilde looked like back in her early thirties. Or maybe late twenties. I'm not sure on that part, but either way, when she was younger."

Unlike me, Taylor had a knack for following convoluted conversations. She immediately grasped the significance of this fact—which I had not when Mathilde phoned me. "Ohmygawd! She's reinvented herself, hasn't she?"

"She so has. Mathilde suffered a serious illness, which resulted in a quick and painless death." I rolled my eyes, because really, how did they get away with that shit? Then again, maybe I'd find out, what with my life now being tied to Dex's. "Her 'granddaughter' inherited her house."

"Nice. Except..." Her lips twisted into a thoughtful pout. "I wonder if this means she'll be dating again."

I wasn't sure what the passing of Mathilde's house to her new self had to do with her dating.

"Oh, honey." Taylor patted my hand. "And you write romance books for a living." She snort-laughed. "Don't glare at me."

I stopped glaring. "I'm not. I just don't see your point. If she wanted to date, she'd have been dating."

And this time it was Taylor rolling her eyes. "As if any woman feels sexy when she's wearing an illusion that ages her fifty-plus years. It's like throwing on your sweats and running outside with your curlers still in. Not sexy, sweetie. Not sexy at all."

I found that analogy offensive to women in general and to women over thirty in particular. I had eye wrinkles and Dex thought I was a babe.

I'd thought Mathilde was smoking from the

instant I met her, smile lines and less-than-perfect skin included.

"Stop frowning so hard. You're missing the point. I'm not saying every woman, whatever her age and appearance, isn't down for some good loving. What I am saying is that you don't exactly go out shopping for a man feeling less than your sexiest self. Mathilde has been wearing a costume for years." She waved her hand. "Whatever. Forget I said anything. It doesn't matter. I don't really care whether your neighbor is getting any or not, as long as she's happy."

I sunk lower in my chair—because was she? Happy? Could she be happy when I sensed a loneliness in her that rivaled my own before I met Dex?

If ever there was a woman calling out for some love—not just loving, aka sexy times—it was my love-witch neighbor.

Dammit. Taylor was right.

But I didn't get a chance to tell her, because Skinny Bitch, aka Susie, had arrived. And, aww, didn't I feel bad now? She looked like a lovely lady.

EPILOGUE: SUSIE

How fucking amazing was it that I'd connected with my fling's ex-fiancée? That was some crazy and ultimately weirdly cool shit.

Even crazier, apparently the mysteriously sexy guy I'd been hooking up with and who was currently fixing Betty, my vintage Bug, was a friend of Dex's. And, wild guess, Bain's as well. If I didn't know better, I'd say there was a man behind the curtain pulling the strings on this one. But both Kaylee and Taylor agreed that the magical community was just that small.

You only realized how small the world was when you'd shared a dick with one of your friends and then realized the current dick in your life was connected to your new friends' dicks.

I'd have to find a new way to explain that if it ever came up in conversation, but I found it satisfying.

As for this magical world they were talking about, it was on my agenda to learn more about it, because, spoiler, I was a witch.

Who knew?

Not my mom. She was one hundred percent human. She also hadn't been on the money with her best guess as to my father's identity. Not the shoe salesman, who had a very boring life with a nice wife and two equally nice kids and most definitely was not a demon. The internet doesn't let anyone keep their secrets, even boring secrets like a wife and two kids.

When I pushed, she backpedaled and said maybe it was that one-night stand she had with that amazingly hot guy that one time...not that she had one-night stands on the regular, because she wasn't that kind of lady. She dated. She didn't have flings. Usually.

I didn't judge my mother for her poor taste in men or even poorer romantic choices. And there were many. So, so many.

She was who she was. She wasn't happy alone,

and that meant that there was a lot of compromising in her life. And a lot of lying, mostly to herself.

It turned out that this little lie she'd told me had backfired, and now I had to figure out what it meant to be a witch.

I guess it was handy that my hookup wasn't just good with cars but also happened to be a dragon.

Thank you for reading *Dragons Do It Nerdier*! I hope you enjoyed Kaylee and Dex's story. They were so much fun to write! I told Kaylee a few times that she needed to go and have amazing dragon sex already, but she kept telling me she wasn't ready yet. And then, wow, I guess they had to make up for it. ;-)

If you haven't already read Bain and Taylor's story, pick up a copy of *Dragons Do It Dirtier* for a fun good-girl, bad-boy-who-isn't-terribly-bad story.

To read about the sexy billionaire dragon (that's Archer!) who pretends to be a mechanic, preorder *Dragons Do It Naughtier*!

I also write flirty, funny vampire romance in the Almost Human Vampire Series. Turn the page for an excerpt from *I Wanna Suck Your...*

I WANNA SUCK YOUR EXCERPT

"I've always wanted to have sex with a vampire."

"Sorry...what?" I flicked back the hood from my Little Red Riding Hood costume and stared at the drunk Jon Snow wannabe standing in front of me.

I'd almost said, "I'm not a vampire." But then that would have been a monstrous lie, and while I might like to suck a little blood from the occasional willing victim, I didn't tell whoppers. It was an arbitrary line to draw, but it was mine.

He flashed his plastic fangs at me. "Decided to come as a vampire instead."

Umkay. Vampiric Jon Snow.

Dick—his name for the night since he was acting

the part—was drunk enough to think he was hilarious. Because *come*.

Yeah. Dick was a winner.

Why was I here again? Oh, right. Megan made
me do it. Damn her. She knows I hate people. Not in
a humans versus vamps kind of way. I'm an equal
opportunity hater. Groups, be they comprised of
humans or vamps, equally repel me.

I'd drawn this conclusion through repeated
observations. Dick was just the latest in a long line of
annoying people who did annoying things.

Time to do the pivot, dodge, and run. It usually
worked well on drunk dudes, because inebriated
men were *slow*.

Also, I was a vampire. A predator. I was fast,
agile, light on my feet.

Usually.

"Oof." All the air in my lungs came out in a noisy
huff when I pivoted right into a wall of man.

A yummy man. Taller than me by a good several
inches, and I'd opted for my bitch boots with the
three-inch block heel this evening, which made me
over five ten. I loved to tower over the little people,
but as I pressed against firm muscles, I decided this
worked, too.

I inhaled. Yeah, I did, because he smelled like

horny heaven, all spicy and clean and masculine... and human.

Nope. I didn't do humans. Why bother? Not like anything could come of it, and there were plenty of vamps happy to get frisky with me.

Only as I moved did I realize the uniquely delicious-smelling human gripped my upper arms with his large hands. All he needed was a little scruff and a deep voice to make me even more pissed off that he was human.

One step back, then another. It took three before I could make eye contact without craning my neck.

And there was the scruff. Damn you, Megan, for making me come to this stupid Halloween party. What kind of damn vampire threw a mixed Halloween party? Who wanted to mingle with their snacks?

Megan. That's who.

"Little Red Riding Hood. Cute."

I was going to stab my best friend. Not in the heart, but this was worth a gaping leg wound.

Over six feet of lean muscle, broad chest, dirty blond scruff covering a sharp jawline, big hands, and a deep, velvety voice.

And human.

I knew exactly how to make Mr. Perfect here less

attractive. I was going to have a conversation that lasted more than three sentences with him. "I was going for the pre-Grimm version."

"Oh?" His gaze traveled up and down my body, just once. Slowly enough so I knew he appreciated what he saw, but without lingering on my breasts. Not bad.

"Pre-Grimm, she saves *herself* from the wolf. No woodsman necessary, thank you very much."

He chuckled, and the velvety smoothness of his voice rubbed against my girly bits in a way that shouldn't have been possible.

Because he was human. This hottie was one hundred percent human, and I was never attracted to humans.

"What's the visual clue that you're not an average, Brothers Grimm sort of Red Riding Hood?"

I shifted my weight so that my hip cocked forward, and smirked. "Do I look like someone who'd get eaten by a wolf?"

He barked out a laugh. "So *you're* what makes the costume badass, not the clingy white T-shirt, the tight black leather pants, or the velvet cloak." He nodded like he agreed.

Smart man.

Wait. Not smart. Just some guy. Some human guy.

Plenty of vamps got a little something-something on the side with humans before they settled down. And I'm sure sex with a human was just fine, but I had a hard enough time dealing with people and their unending irritating habits. Asking me to put forth the effort of spending more than fifteen minutes with a man who had zero chance of being my bonded mate? No thanks.

This guy, though, he was making me rethink the idea of casual sex with no possibility of mating.

Probably a good idea to haul ass before that happened. I was about to make my excuses when he held out his hand. "Simon."

I couldn't *not* shake it. Not when it gave me an opportunity to fondle his large palm and his long thick fingers.

Goddess. I needed to get laid. I was thinking porny thoughts about the man's hand. And not giving it back to him.

Not that he was complaining.

"Becca."

"Really nice to meet you, Becca. How do you know Megan?" He was still holding onto my hand. It seemed he was just as happy to maintain contact as I was.

"That evil bitch is my best friend. You?"

He arched his eyebrows. "Work. Any particular reason you sound like you'd like to give her a black eye?"

"There's more blood in my version. And a knife." I rolled my eyes and reclaimed my hand. "She made me come tonight."

"And you're having a terrible time." His lips quirked with amusement. Not bad, Simon. Most guys' fragile egos couldn't take the slightest hint that they weren't the queso and chips of every woman's world.

Speaking of... "Have you seen the queso? I was promised spicy cheese and plentiful tortilla chips. And margaritas. Where the hell are the margaritas?" But then I realized he'd implied, if not outright asked, a question. I stopped my long-distance scan of the spread in Megan's kitchen (I hadn't made it past the living room) and turned to Simon. With all of my attention on him, I said, "Yes, I was having a shit time. Dick was hitting on me, and there are no drinks in my hands."

"Dick?"

"Jon Snow, vampire style."

Simon chuckled again. "Man, that's weird. You have to mean Robert. He's the only Jon Snow here, but I didn't catch the vampire part. That guy..."

"Better be single, or he's losing a testicle tonight."

"Very. Not that it's an excuse for bad behavior, but he's normally a moderately respectful man." He looked over my shoulder in the general vicinity of Dick's last sighting. "When he's not wasted."

Before I could affirm that Dick—apparently a work colleague of Simon and Megan's named Robert —was indeed wasted tonight, Simon cupped my elbow with that large, warm hand of his. Dammit. I was overdue some sexy times, because it was downright unnatural for me to be lusting after a human, and weirder yet that I was having porny thoughts about his hands.

"I'm afraid you've missed the queso, but I can lead you to the secret margarita stash."

It wasn't secret. The massive, well-stocked bar was out on the patio and even had its very own bartender. Late October in Austin was hardly frigid, and tonight was actually perfect for patio loitering. I just hadn't made it that far before being waylaid by Dick. Minus the queso shortage and her guest list—which included people, so not much to be done about it—Megan knew how to throw a good party. We'd have words about the lack of queso.

Simon presented the bar with an outstretched hand. "I'm guessing you don't come to many of these, since I've never met you and the bar is always out back, even in questionable weather."

"Nope. I hate people."

He cocked his head as if confused—he shouldn't be; I hadn't hid anything about my personality and all its quirks—then said, "Only in the collective sense, or individuals, as well?"

"Oh, good question, Simon." I couldn't resist saying his name. I liked it, with its old-fashioned feel. I'd never met a Simon, not that I could remember. "I'm equally disenchanted with individuals and groups, but for different reasons."

His lips twitched as he ordered two margaritas from the bartender and asked for two shots of tequila, as well. Once the cute twenty-something behind the bar peeled her eyes off him and started making our drinks, he said, "Educate me. Give me your top three list for groups and individuals."

"My top three list?"

"Sure. The three things you hate most about people in their singular and collective capacities."

This guy was dangerous. He didn't blink at my

misanthropic tendencies, and he made my girly parts take notice. Down, tiger.

"Only three, huh? I hate that people in crowds act like Dick."

"Robert."

"Yeah, that guy. Maybe he has some degree of social anxiety and feels the need to lubricate at these events, or maybe he knows social standards are loosened in large groups and he just likes the excuse to be a dick."

Point in Simon's favor, he did not giggle when the word "lubricate" slipped past my gaudy red lips. "There will always be the Dicks of the world, but that's only one."

Then again, Simon wasn't really a giggle kind of guy. He was more a "chuckle in that deep sexy way that made me shiver." Oh, yeah, and wet. The mellow tones of his voice were definitely causing a party in my pants.

"Ah, don't worry. I have more." I glanced at the two shots that had appeared as we'd chatted. The margaritas were still getting mixed. Our bartender had been multitasking, handing out beer and wine as she made our drinks. Fair enough. There was brisk traffic chez Megan this evening.

Following my gaze, Simon discovered the shots

and a sexy grin appeared. Offering me one, he held the other in his hand and lifted it. "To avoiding the Dicks of the world."

Now that I could drink to.

I welcomed the burn of the liquor. Maybe it would drown out some of the ridiculous thoughts I was having about the human standing a foot away from me.

Because tequila did that: it chased away bad decisions. That earned a mental eye roll. But my recognition of the evils of tequila and its impact on my ability to think critically didn't stop me from toasting the other five things I hated about people, singularly and collectively.

And bam! I was drunk. Just like that.

To be fair, six shots and three margaritas later wasn't exactly sudden drunkenness. But time with Simon flew by. However long it took a horny misanthropic vampire to drink six shots and three margaritas, that was how long it took for me to fall completely in lust with Simon Fullerton, engineer, runner, shirt-tucker, and guy whose presence didn't annoy me beyond tolerance.

That last one was kind of a shocker.

I kept expecting the next words out of his mouth

to be the ones that tipped the scales to "and now I want to smack you."

But it kept not happening.

And this from a guy who wore a pressed button-down to a Halloween party. I had to ask. "You're not in costume, are you?"

"No." His smile turned sheepish. "This is how I dress."

Jeans in good repair that fit nicely over his firm ass, a pressed shirt stretched across his strong chest and tucked neatly into his jeans, a belt that matched his shoes, and the occasional peek of socks that coordinated with his shirt. He wasn't a fashionable guy. He looked good, but I didn't get the impression he'd given a lot of thought to his attire. His clothes fit, were in good repair, and all matched in some way.

Simon made it startlingly clear that I'd been surrounding myself with man-child men. I'd hit my thirties and subconsciously expected the men around me to act differently. Spoiler: they hadn't. Most of them still wore threadbare band tees and faded jeans. Or skinny jeans. Or shorts with flip flops. Welcome to the life of a creative, filled with other creatives.

But Simon didn't fit that mold. He wasn't a

creative. He wore grown-up clothes...that he apparently ironed. And I *still* wasn't finding him annoying.

I blamed Simon's sheepish smile for what happened next.

Also the booze, but it was the smile that really pushed my buttons.

Warning, warning. Danger ahead. Drunk vampire at a party with a hot human guy.

Warnings were for other people.

I leaned in, wrapped my hand around the back of his neck (not *just* so I wouldn't fall over), and tipped my chin up.

A set of very interested blue eyes looked down at me.

And then he kissed me.

TO KEEP READING, pick up your copy of *I Wanna Suck Your!*

ABOUT THE AUTHOR

Fanglicious! That's Gemma Cates.

She writes flirty shifter and vampire romances with plenty of the steamy stuff and a solid dash of humor. If you're looking for hot paranormal fun, fangs, and laughter, she's happy to oblige.

When Gemma's not cooking up happily-ever-afters for her heroes and heroines, she might be writing books in other, sweeter genres. (She'll never tell.)

For release announcements and more, subscribe to her newsletter on her website: www.Gemma-Cates.com

Printed in Great Britain
by Amazon